THE MIRACLE *in* CHARLIE'S WOODS

George Reker
960 Maple Lane
Hanover, Pa. 17331
george-Reker@comcast.net
717-688-4162

THE MIRACLE
in
CHARLIE'S WOODS

GEORGE REIKER

FOREWORD BY JASON LILLER

Stock Street Press

Stock Street Press
960 Maple Lane
Hanover, PA 17331

ISBN: 978-0-578-91950-8

Library of Congress Control Number: 2021939526

Contact the author at ReikerBooks@Gmail.com

FOREWORD

BY JASON LILLER

Some stories have the power to change the global course of human events. Some change the fate of nations. Some stories change only a single life but create ripples that echo into eternity.

George Reiker has written just such a story, and no wonder: Recreated in these pages is Charlie "Tremendous" Jones, a remarkable, real-life person who changed countless lives, including mine.

I met Charlie "Tremendous" Jones (so named because, as he put it, he had a limited vocabulary and exclaimed *Tremendous!* at every piece of news, good or bad) in 1999 in Mechanicsburg, Pennsylvania. He gave me a colossal bear hug and said, "You're Jason Liller? *The* Jason Liller? Do you know how many people spend their whole lives waiting to *meet* you?"

I was no one important (or so I thought), but Charlie didn't see it that way. With just a few words he brightened my day and elevated my mood. He made me feel like the two of us were the only people on the planet. I soon realized that this was his standard greeting—he greeted virtually everyone exactly the way he had greeted me, but that only emphasizes my point: He brightened *everyone's* day, he elevated *everyone's* mood, he made *everyone* feel important, and he did it without focusing on himself. He *never* focused on himself. He focused on *you.* And his words could change your life.

I watched Charlie save marriages, rejuvenate careers, rehabilitate the downtrodden, and rescue those who had lost their faith. People from across the world sought his advice and counsel, and he made time for them all. He shared his wisdom with a reassuring, grandfatherly tone and a sense of moral authority that few people could muster, but he never took the credit for what he did. He maintained that he was a conduit for Jesus Christ, and he saw to it that this fact was lost on no one. When you met Charlie Jones you met the best example of a Christ-centered person leading a Christ-centered life and he made you want to live the same way. He evangelized by example and he was irresistible.

If there is one disappointing thing about Charlie Jones it's this: He passed away (or *went home*, as Charlie would say) in 2008 and too many people didn't get the chance to meet him. George Reiker has done us all a great favor by bringing Charlie Jones back to life in these pages—a fictionalized version of the man, yes, and in a fictional setting—but with his essence so true that his voice rings clearly from George's words. Charlie Jones is waiting to meet *you,* and he will change your life just as he changed mine. Take the journey. Turn the page.

Trust the Lord thy God with all your heart and lean not unto your own understanding but acknowledge him in all your ways and surely he will direct your path.

—Proverbs 3:5-6

PART ONE

PART ONE

CHAPTER ONE

My childhood was stolen at the tender age of eleven. My mother's sudden death shattered my childhood and led me into a disastrous marriage which ended in divorce, followed by another relationship that ended badly, forcing me to question everything I thought I knew about myself. The depth of my despair and loneliness was truly frightening.

I was on my own raising Brent, my ten-year-old son. My love for him gave me the courage to pick myself up and face an uncertain future even when I otherwise felt like quitting. My total focus was on raising my son and any thought of getting into another relationship was pushed out of my mind. I turned the matter of finding true love over to God. I didn't have much faith in him, but it was obvious that my own choices had been terrible.

So I wasn't interested when Kim, a friend of mine, tried to introduce me to someone. The last thing I needed was to meet another woman. No, I was happy on my own with my son. Just leave me alone.

Over the next six months Kim would casually sneak in this blind-date business. "Ryan, you should just meet her. She's such a lovely woman, I know you'd like her." My response was always the same: *I'm not interested in a relationship. I'm still hurting from the last disaster.*

I used to think I understood women. In fact, it was a point of pride for me. I tried to be sensitive to their wants and desires. In high school, some of my closest friends were girls. I was always someone they could talk to and trust. I became a great listener. Now, years later, I realize they were helping me as much as I was helping them. I was drowning in a horrible and abusive relationship with my stepmother at home, so listening to their problems helped take my mind off my own.

But after the failure of a ten-year marriage and my disastrous relationship with Debra, I no longer trusted my insights or intuition. I was so low it took all my strength just to care for my son. There just wasn't anything left to give to anyone else.

Kim, dear friend that she was, understood everything I was going through. I think she knew I would never meet anyone on my own, so she just kept nudging. Slowly, my inner self healed and my bruised heart recovered. So on that evening, when Kim stopped by for a visit, I finally gave in. I had drowned in self-pity long enough. It was time to move on.

I told her I was ready to meet her friend, Sarah, if she was still interested. But, I stressed, it was only for friendship, nothing more.

"I know, I know. I can't wait to ask tomorrow. You'll see I'm right about her," Kim teased. "How's lunch at Rio Pub—say Friday?"

"That's fine with me. Just let me know."

As Kim drove away down the tree-lined drive, I could only stand and shake my head. *I hope I know what I'm doing. Ah, it's just a lunch.*

I pulled into Rio's parking lot that Friday and looked for the blue Pontiac Grand Prix Kim said Sarah drove. It was early—11:30—and the lunch crowd hadn't arrived yet. Of the several cars in the lot, none were Sarah's. I parked in a space and nervously waited. It was a gorgeous fall day—sunny, upper sixties, and the scents of fall filled the air. As I sat there lightly tapping my fingers to the music on the radio, I wondered what she would be like. Could Sarah be as wonderful as Kim said? Could this be a new start?

"Hi. Are you Ryan Samuels?"

Her voice snapped me out of my thoughts. I never saw her pull next to me. "Yes, I am. You must be Sarah."

"Yes, it's nice to meet you finally," she said. "I've heard so much about you.

"Me, too. I guess Kim's been keeping both of us informed."

"I know what you mean. I don't think either of us could have gotten out of this."

As we walked into the restaurant, we kidded each other about the situation Kim had put us in. After we were seated, I had my first chance to really look at her. Sarah was slender with beautiful auburn hair that hung over her shoulders. And her voice was soft and gentle. My first impression set me at ease. We ordered food and wine and the conversation flowed effortlessly between us like a gentle stream. Oh, we covered the usual topics a man and woman usually do when they first meet: our work, our children, movies, and so on. Sarah owned an interior decorating business that she had started four years ago, after her divorce. I also learned she had two daughters—Lindsey and Elisha. Lindsey was thirteen and special needs. She had been born premature and has cerebral palsy. Everything Sarah said about Lindsey was filled with love and devotion. Elisha was ten and apparently quite the little girl. I could see the love and pride in Sarah's eyes as she showed me their pictures.

I told her about Brent, and that I'd been a single father for six years. I shared my own photos and, before we realized it, two hours had passed. Sarah was so easy to talk to.

Since we both had to return to work, we paid our check and walked out to our cars. "Ryan, I didn't want to admit this, but I really enjoyed our lunch and I felt so at ease talking to you. I just want you to know how refreshing our conversation was."

We exchanged phone numbers and I told her I would call. As she got in her car, she looked up. "I sense that you're the kind gentleman Kim described—and quite handsome, too," she said with a little laugh. Then she pulled away before I could reply.

"Why, thank you," I yelled after her. I got in my car with a sensation of happiness that I hadn't felt in a long time. I rested my head on the steering wheel, over-whelmed with the feeling. It had been so long since the gray skies of despair and unhappiness had fallen over me. This burst of unexpected sunshine was like releasing a pressure valve on my emotions. Tears forced themselves to the surface. I couldn't wait to see her again.

CHAPTER TWO

Saturday morning I woke up feeling surprisingly refreshed. Pictures of yesterday's lunch kept floating in my mind while I sipped my fresh-brewed coffee.

I reflected on yesterday's lunch as I sat on the back patio in the early sun. I could still see Sarah in her flowing green dress. She looked so lovely. She had made quite an impression. But even as I enjoyed the memories of our lunch, I couldn't afford the luxury of getting carried away in the moment. *Maybe we could develop a nice friendship. No danger in that.*

Sunday night came and I hesitated calling Sarah. I knew I had to—how would it look if I didn't? But in my mind each meeting or conversation was a step toward a relationship. As I dialed her number, anxiety crept in. My nerves eased at the sound of her soft *hello*. Again, the conversation flowed. We talked for hours. Afterward, I sat in silence, amazed. *What is going on here?* I felt like I was slowly being put under a spell. *One day at a time.*

Several weeks passed before we saw each other again. My job as a sales rep for Mercor Corporation took me to Indiana for a three-day business trip. We sold video-conferencing equipment and my territory was taking off. Also, taking care of Brent didn't leave much leisure time. Sarah, with two girls and her decorating business, was in the same situation, especially with Lindsey. We did manage a phone call or two, but it wasn't enough. When I finally had a break in my schedule I invited her over to my place for a Saturday dinner. Sarah's girls were with their dad, and Brent was with his mom, so it was a perfect opportunity.

I enjoyed cooking. Being a single father, I was quite good at domestic duties. My friends always teased that I'd make a good wife. I got up early so I could pick up the ingredients for the evening's meal: a nice piece of salmon, and some clams to steam for an appetizer. I also picked up some asparagus and a few other essentials before heading back home. As I carried the groceries to the door, Red, my Irish Setter, welcomed me home with his frantic, friendly barks. Red has been with me thirteen years now, and he especially loved me when I brought food home. "Yes, I got you something," I shouted as I put the bags on the counter. I let him bark and wag his tail for a few minutes before I finally gave in and gave him his treat. I scratched him behind the ears. We've developed a strong and loving bond.

After the groceries were put away, Red and I went to the back patio to take in the freshness of the morning. The sun had already started to chase away the chill. I sat back in a lounge, patting Red, and slowly breathed in the crisp, fresh air. I relished the seclusion and privacy of the nineteen acres that I called home even though it took every cent I had to acquire it. Birds were singing and, far in the distance, the sound of a neighbor's lawn mower.

This was my time to reflect. These still morning moments were my lifeline in times of despair. They helped keep me from drowning. As I closed my eyes, I let everything slip away, emptying my mind of all distractions. I found it utterly amazing that less than a year ago I toyed with the thought of killing myself. Red sensed the change in my mood and laid his head on my lap. I stroked his head. *It's okay, boy. I'm all right now, no need to worry.* My mind turned to the evening's dinner. I was slowly letting go of my resistance, or maybe Sarah was charming it out of me. Whatever the reason, I looked forward to a nice relaxing dinner.

Sarah pulled up to the house as I walked in from the garden. I waved, almost dropping a basket of vegetables. "Hi," I said. "Welcome to my humble abode."

She was radiant, dressed in an ivory sweater and faded jeans. Red came barking.

"He's okay," I shouted. "He likes people and I told him all about you."

She laughed as she knelt down to pet him, his tail wagging. "I think he likes you," I said.

"Oh, he is such a pretty dog. How old did you say he is?"

"Thirteen," I answered.

"He's so friendly."

We went into the house, Red bouncing after us, and settled in the kitchen. "Would you like some wine?" I asked.

"Sure would. Vino is keeno" Her response brought a smile to my face as I poured her a glass. May I help with anything?"

I shook my head. "No, just relax and enjoy your vino. I said with a wink."

She watched me for a moment as I worked in the kitchen, then she gazed around the room. "You must have a green thumb with all these house plants."

I smiled and raised my thumb. She laughed. "When we finish dinner, I'll show you around outside if you'd like," I said.

With soft music playing in the background, I was truly enjoying my dinner date. "Everything is delicious," she said. "You're quite the cook."

"Thank you," I answered. "When you're a single parent you'd better learn to cook or eat out a lot. And Brent does like most of what I cook. How does he put it? Oh, yes. 'Dad, you make good stuff.'"

After dinner we loaded the dishwasher and stepped outside. Red had taken an immediate liking to Sarah, prancing happily beside her. The air was sharp with the aromas of autumn and though the trees were still full of color, their leaves had started to speckle the ground.

"Thank you for a lovely dinner," Sarah said softly. "I can tell you went to a lot of trouble. I'm not used to having a man cook for me."

"Oh, it was no trouble at all. In fact, I really enjoyed doing it."

We followed the path to a little pond where the fiery red glow of the setting sun was reflected in the water. We stopped for a second to take in the view, Sarah beside me, appreciating the beauty of the moment. "I find peace and solitude out here," I said. We walked around the the pond to the edge of the woods. Red spotted a rabbit and took off after it as fast as his old legs could go, barking all the way. "Red likes it, too," I joked. We both laughed. It felt so good to laugh again.

As we slowly wandered back to the house I reached over and took Sarah's hand. I breathed a sigh of relief as her fingers wrapped around mine. A chill filled the air as the sun dipped below the horizon. I said, "I can build a fire inside, or we can make one outside. Which would you prefer?"

Sarah thought for a moment. "Outside. It'll feel like we're camping and I like camping."

"Camping it will be," I said.

Soon the fire was blazing and we sat side by side sipping coffee.

"The fire feels nice, Ryan, thank you. Thank you for everything. You know, I can't even remember the last time I had such a relaxing evening."

As I listened to her words I realized how good I felt, too, and how much I enjoyed her company. Her genuine caring and love for life seemed a natural part of her. The joy she got from nature, her affection for animals, the glow that radiated from her when she talked about her children—dare I even think she might be God's answer to my prayers? I had made so many bad choices, I had finally surrendered this to him.

"Ryan, hello!" Then I saw her hand waving in front of me, jerking me away from my thoughts.

"I'm sorry. I kind of got lost in my thoughts."

"Oh, that's okay. I was temporarily lost in mine, too." She reached over and grabbed my hand. "Anything you care to talk about?"

"I just realized what a wonderful time I'm having and how easy it is to be with you. I haven't felt like this in a very long time."

She looked into my eyes as if searching my soul. "I feel the same way, but part of me doesn't want to admit it. I feel so comfortable just being next to you. I can't even explain it, but it's nice."

I put my arm around her and pulled her close. We sat there just holding each other. The sensation I felt between us was so serene. She leaned back into my arms. We sat for a long time, staring into the fire, its flames dancing in the darkness, each in our own thoughts, content in the moment.

Finally, Sarah said she had to be going. I walked her to her car and opened the door. "Thanks, Ryan, again, for a lovely evening." She stood on her toes and kissed my cheek. "You are a true gentleman, you made tonight very special." She gave me her big warm smile as she climbed into her car. "Call me," she said, and sped down the lane. I looked down at Red and said, "Hmm, I may have to install a speed bump or two for her," I chuckled.

Red and I walked back and sat by the fire. I glanced at my watch. It was 11:30. I sat there for another hour or so, lost in my thoughts of the evening. I finally put out the fire. As I slowly undressed for bed, my mind was still on Sarah. She seemed too good to be true. I put my head on the pillow and stared at the ceiling, struggling with my feelings and my actions. I couldn't let this be anything more than a friendship. I had to keep my feelings under control. I had no choice. I felt my very survival depended on it.

I tossed and turned and wondered if Sarah was thinking the same thoughts.

CHAPTER THREE

Red's barking ended my slumber. The brightness of the sun shining through my bedroom window made me turn over and bury my head under the blanket. But Red persisted, pulling the covers off to the side of the bed. "Okay, boy, okay. Do you need to go out that bad?" That question hit the mark as his barking and prancing quickened. I slipped on my sweatpants, hurried downstairs, and opened the back door. Red bolted outside. "Sorry if I was slow this morning, boy," I yelled after him, laughing.

As I headed into the house, I realized how much my relationship with Debra had changed me. *How sad that life's tough lessons harden our hearts.* While I was happy with my feelings for Sarah, I knew how guarded I was of those feelings. I wondered how much life's hard knocks had changed me. Could I openly love another woman? Would the shadows of the past, and its soul-wrenching heartbreaks, cloud my ability to love anew? I knew that Sarah and I had some major obstacles to overcome if our relationship was to ever blossom into something more than friendship.

I picked Brent up from his mother's on Sunday evening. We laughed and kidded each other on the drive home. "What did you do this weekend?" I asked.

"We went to the zoo and Mom let me have a friend over, too. There were lots of animals, even lions and tigers."

"Wow," I said. "I bet you had a good time."

"We did. Oh, we saw polar bears, too. They're really big." I laughed at his excitement.

Red gave us his usual heartfelt greeting as I opened the car door, barking and running back and forth. He ran after Brent as he took his things up to his room. I laid out a washcloth and towel and called after him, "Brent, you need to get your bath."

"Okay, Dad. Hey, can I play my new video game when I'm done?" he asked.

"Okay, but just for fifteen or twenty minutes." I walked down to the kitchen to make some tea. The night air was cool, so I started a fire in the fireplace. I looked forward to relaxing in front of it. After I finished my tea, I went upstairs to tuck my son into bed. "It's a neat game, Dad. It's really cool."

"Ready for bed?" I asked. "Teeth brushed?"

"Yes, all done."

I pulled the covers up over him as he climbed into bed. He giggled and I gave him a kiss on the cheek. "I love you, son," I said.

"I love you, too, Dad."

"Sweet dreams," I said as I walked to the door and turned off the light. He turned away and shuffled under the covers. I stood at the door, soaking in the moment. Looking at his little body snuggled peacefully in his bed, my heart swelled with love and satisfaction. He was the focus of my life, he meant everything to me. I lightly closed his door and went back downstairs to put on some soft music and sit by the fire. Red, of course, was right beside me. I leaned my head back against the couch and took a deep breath. It had been a busy weekend and all the activity had left me tired.

I thought of Brent and all we had been through together. He was such a tremendous help to me and he seemed to have adjusted remarkably well. For a ten-year-old he was mature past his years, kind, thoughtful, and respectful. I loved him with all of my being. And it hurt because, despite his laughter and happiness, I knew the divorce had wounded him deeply. I still felt guilty about my relationship with Debra and the disaster it turned out to be. He seemed always understanding and even sympathetic. I can still remember, after one of our talks, him looking up at me and saying, "It's okay, Dad. I want you to be happy. We'll be okay." As on that night, I found myself crying now. I wiped my tears away, surprised by the rush of emotion. Red laid his head on my lap, sensing my pain. I patted his head and smiled. "Where would I be without both of you?" His tail wagged in approval.

My thoughts turned again to Sarah. She was so different from any woman I had ever met. I enjoyed being with her, but a relationship scared me. I couldn't put Brent or myself through another bad one. I tossed this around in my thoughts for what seemed like hours, and then I finally went to bed.

November sped by quickly and Sarah and I found our time gobbled up by work and single parenthood. We

did manage to see each other a few times, and our friendship steadily grew. The conversations we shared became
more open and always honest. We realized that we had
much in common and shared many principles of life. We
were developing a special friendship and we both sensed
we were headed for waters neither of us wanted to wade
into: *a relationship*. The R-word had become a dreaded
word for both of us.

We were amazed by how our lives paralleled one
another. Sarah's first marriage was to an abusive and
overbearing husband. Even though married, she raised
her children alone, and the special care that Lindsey
needed . . . well, I truly admired Sarah for her love and
commitment. I never heard a complaint or a word of self-
pity. I tried to come to terms with the haunting facts of a
special needs child. Could I handle that? Why would I
choose that awesome responsibility if I could just walk
away?

It was somewhat easy up to this point to dismiss
these thoughts because Sarah and I had kept our children
out of our budding friendship. This was about to change.
Sarah invited Brent and I over for dinner to meet Lindsey
and Elisha. After I accepted, I couldn't stop questioning

myself. *What was I doing?* Having our children meet would be a definite step towards a deeper relationship.

I was terrified. *I can't do this. I'm not ready. And what if it doesn't work out? How would Brent react?* I felt like a scared child, cornered, trembling with fear. I had never experienced anything like it before. I was paralyzed by the reality of the repercussions this dinner could have.

As Saturday approached, I thought of all kinds of excuses for not going. I picked up the phone, but never made the call. When Saturday came, I felt I had no choice but to go. I kept telling myself, *It'll be all right.* With a deep breath I started the car. My son and I were on our way.

CHAPTER FOUR

As we drove to Sarah's, I again assured Brent how nice Sarah was, and how thoughtful it was of her to have us over for dinner. I had discussed all this with him earlier, and I told him about Elisha and Lindsey and tried to explain Lindsey's condition based on what Sarah had shared told me. I showed him their picture. "Those are Sarah's daughters."

"Doesn't she have any boys?" he asked.

"No, just girls."

"Okay," he said, disappointed. "I guess I can play with girls."

I had to chuckle.

It was early December and it was almost dark when we pulled into Sarah's driveway. She lived in a nice, two-story Victorian-style house on the edge of town. A cold breeze greeted us as strolled up the front walk.

I took a deep breath and knocked. Elisha, Sarah's ten-year-old, swung open the door. "They're here! They're here!" she yelled.

The aromas of dinner filled the air. A fireplace crackled in the living room. Sarah took our coats and introduced us to Lindsey and Elisha. Brent wasn't sure what to make of Lindsey; he offered a shaky hello. She sat in a chair in the living room, rocking back and forth. I knelt and said hello. Lindsey gave us a quick glance as if to say *Who are you?* then looked away, still rocking.

"I don't think she likes us," Brent said, nudging up against me. "She didn't say hi or anything."

"Remember . . ." I started to explain.

Sarah came to my rescue. "Brent," she said softly as she knelt beside him, "Lindsey can talk, but not the way you and I do. She talks in lots of ways, you just need to learn what they are."

I stood back and watched the loving and gentle way she talked to Brent. He hung on every word she said.

The love and compassion that flowed from her was as natural as breathing. She was a sight to behold.

Sarah gave me a tour of her home while Elisha took Brent off to show him her room. Downstairs beside the living room was a large country kitchen, Lindsey and Sarah's bedrooms, and a bath. Upstairs were two large rooms that Elisha claimed as her own. "We'll eat in about fifteen minutes," she said. "Would you like a glass of wine before dinner?"

"Sure. Sounds good," I answered. I needed something to calm my nerves.

"Was Brent nervous about coming?" she asked.

"No, not really. I think I was more nervous than he was."

Sara laughed. "Why?"

"I'm not sure, really, but I'm okay." She handed me a glass and I took a sip. "You have a lovely place, Sarah. You and the girls seem very happy."

"We are. We're very content here."

"If it's okay to ask, what did you say Lindsey's condition is?" I asked, trying to find the right words.

31

"She was born about two months premature with cerebral palsy and, during her birth, her breathing stopped, causing damage to her brain. That's why she's unable to walk or talk. She's been such a blessing in our lives, though."

Her words amazed me. *A blessing.* I'm ashamed to say so, but I found it difficult to understand Sarah's comment.

We ate supper and Elisha and Brent got along great, but Elisha did most of the jabbering. I watched Sarah as she fed Lindsey who, I observed, did not maintain eye contact with anyone for longer than a few seconds, just an occasional look and then back to her world. I watched the communication between mother and daughter and how Sarah knew how to make Lindsey respond. At first Brent and I weren't sure how to react, but when Sarah and Elisha laughed, we laughed too.

Dinner was both delicious and relaxing. We all helped clean off the table when Sarah announced dessert. "Apple dumplings and ice cream," she said. "Who would like some?"

"I'll have some," Elisha chimed back.

"Me, too," Brent added, his eyes wide with anticipation. I laughed to myself. Though I was a decent cook, I didn't bake much. This would be a treat for both of us.

After dessert, we went to the living room to watch a movie with the kids. I couldn't help but notice how well Elisha and Brent got along, the way they played together. You would have thought they had been friends for years. Part way through the movie, Lindsey let Sarah know she was ready for bed.

Though Lindsey was small for thirteen, she was still quite a load to carry around. I watched as Sarah picked her up and out of her chair. We all said goodnight as they disappeared down the hall. I sat there amazed at Sarah's graceful way with her. My respect and admiration continually grew. The genuine love that flowed between mother and daughters tugged at my heart.

My concerns about Sarah being real were slowly disappearing. When she returned from putting Lindsey to bed and sat next to me on the couch. We talked quietly while Elisha and Brent watched the rest of the movie. She shared how Lindsey communicated her wants and needs. I could see in her eyes the sense of joy she felt caring for her girls. "What?" she asked, noticing my expression.

"I'm just amazed, Sarah. I don't know what else to say, just purely amazed."

"At what?" she asked.

"Your whole attitude, the way you handle being a single parent, how happy and content you seem."

"You noticed all that in one evening?"

"Well," I said, smiling, "I'm very observant."

"Well, what about you?" she asked. "You and Brent seem to have a wonderful relationship."

"Oh, you're observant, too," I joked.

We laughed, apparently too loudly, because Elisha turned around with her finger pressed to her lips. It only made us laugh more.

After the movie, Elisha wanted to go up to her room and play. I told Brent it was okay, but we'd be leaving in about an hour. Off they ran, giggling the whole way up the stairs.

"Well, we finally have a little time to ourselves," I said.

We exchanged our first real kiss that evening, one that neither of us would forget. As our lips touched, electricity seemed to fill the air, our passion unleashed, mouths pressed together, adrenaline rushing. When we finally separated, we each had to catch our breath. For a second we just looked into each other's eyes. Then a grin spread across her face, and I felt myself blush.

Brent and Elisha ran down the stairs and interrupted our moment. I told Brent we had to be going. As I stood, still light-headed from the kiss, I knelt down and said good night to Elisha and told her how nice it was to finally meet her. I stood and thanked Sarah for a wonderful dinner. I gave her a hug and she whispered in my ear, "That was a great kiss, Mr. Samuels." We looked into each other's eyes and knew that tonight thrust us into forbidden territory. Though neither of us wanted a serious relationship, that no longer mattered. Love had wrapped her arms around us and there was no escaping. As Brent and I walked to our car I had a feeling our lives would never be the same.

CHAPTER FIVE

Sunday morning was cloudy and chilly. Brent and I ate breakfast and got dressed for church. It had been quite some time since we had gone, but on this morning something prompted me to make the effort. As we drove, our conversation was filled with the coming of Christmas. Brent cheerfully announced he was already preparing his list. I smiled at his childish enthusiasm.

Rain started to fall as we got closer to town. "I can't wait for snow," Brent said.

"I hope it snows for Christmas," I added. "How did you like dinner last night?"

"It was really good, except for the green beans. But I love the apple dumplings with ice cream. Sarah's a good cook."

"Yes, she is. You seemed to like everyone."

"They were nice," he replied. "And it was fun hanging around Elisha, even if she is a girl," He looked out the window at the streaking raindrops. "Lindsey has lots of problems, doesn't she?"

"We may see them as problems," I said, "but I don't think Sarah does."

"She's really nice."

"That she is, son."

We arrived at church and took our seats. Brent especially loved the singing. He always made me so proud. As the minister started his sermon, I sensed a strong presence around us. Then a voice spoke to me. *Stay true to the path I've put you on. Trust in me.* I sat perfectly still. Who was speaking? I looked around. No one was paying any attention to me.

The rest of the service was a blur. I couldn't get the voice, or its message, out of my head. *Stay true to the path I've put you on. Trust in me. What does it mean? What path? Must have been my imagination.*

The rain had stopped. On the way home I told Brent what had happened. He looked at me with innocent, loving eyes. "Do you think it was God?"

His question surprised me. "Why would he talk to *me?*"

"He talks to me sometimes."

"He does? Well, I guess he can talk to me, too."

After we got home, Brent went in the den and played. I started a fire and sat down to think. I asked God to help me know which path he wanted me to stay true to. I had no sooner finished when the phone rang. It was Sarah. She wanted to know if we enjoyed dinner and if I was nervous now that the children had met. I knew she was concerned, and I told her I was still pretty calm about everything. She laughed. We talked for a while and made plans to get together next weekend. As we said our goodbyes, I had a sudden urge to say *I love you.* I fought the impulse and quickly hung up. *Are you crazy?* Then my mind ceased those thoughts, replaced by a new one: *Trust in me.* What did it mean? Why was this voice talking to me?

Even though I believed in God, we hadn't enjoyed an ongoing close relationship. Oh, I turned to him in my times of need, but I would also throw my hands up in disgust because of all my tragedies and heartaches. My faith at best was on unstable ground. I often believed God had abandoned me. Months would go by before I would discover how wrong I had been.

Sarah and I talked several more times that week. Our relationship grew deeper with each moment we shared. We decided to get together over the weekend and openly talk about how we wanted our relationship to proceed. The children would be at their other parents, so it would be a good opportunity, but part of me dreaded it.

Sarah arrived around seven o'clock on Saturday evening. It had snowed the night before, just enough to cover the trees and grassy areas, and she commented on how beautiful everything looked. I took her coat and we sat in the living room by the fire. "You use your fireplace a great deal," she said.

"Every day if I can," I replied.

There was a warm glow in the room. The light from the fire bathed the walls and ceiling in flickering patterns of light. I put on some tea and some relaxing music. "I figure we can use all the ambiance we can for this evening," I teased.

She smiled and nodded her approval. As I poured the tea we discussed our plans for Christmas, and the joy we shared in watching the excitement of the children. I handed her a cup and gave her a light kiss on her cheek. She gave me a loving look and motioned for me to sit next to her. I obliged. She took a sip from her cup.

I took a deep breath and said, "I know we need to have this discussion. Where do we start?"

"Oh, there's no particular place to start. Let's just express our feelings, you know, let's just be honest," she said as she gently put her hands in mine.

"I'll let you go first since I'm a *gentleman*." I smiled, lightening the mood temporarily.

"Ryan, I know neither of us intended to get seriously involved, but somehow it has happened."

"I know," I said.

"I want you to know that there's no pressure to go on if you feel at any time you're not ready." I listened intently, the gentleness of her voice relaxing me. "I've fallen in love with you, and many times I just wanted to turn and run. You scare me."

"I *scare* you? But why?" I asked.

"Because of everything I'm experiencing. I'm realizing you are the first man I have ever truly opened my heart to and it frightens me. I know how much you can hurt me."

She shushed me when I tried to respond. "Until now I'd never let a man totally into my heart. Before I even realized it you had opened a door that I had kept closed. I can't fight back my feelings for you." She stopped for a moment to collect her emotions.

"Sarah, I never meant for any of this to happen. In fact, I've wanted to run the other way myself."

"I sensed that," she replied. "That's why I thought we should have this talk before we go any further."

"I agree. Because we have other people to consider, not just ourselves." I respected her honesty and her compassion. She said everything I was thinking.

I allowed her to continue. "Whenever I see you, you literally take my breath away. And when you wrap your arms around me I feel safe and secure." There was a glow around her as she poured her heart out. I was deeply touched and moved. "Ryan, I am happy, or thought I was, just me and my girls. Life was good and then you came along."

"Well, thanks," I said dejectedly.

"You know what I mean."

"Yes, but I can't help but tease you a little."

She sipped her tea while I put more wood on the fire. "I really appreciate your honesty, Sarah," I said. "It's refreshing and something that's been lacking from the women I've been involved with." I sat back down and gave her a hug. There were tears in her eyes. "Are you okay?" I asked.

"I'm fine, I'm fine," she replied. "I promised myself I wouldn't cry. See what you do to me?" she said with a little smile.

I shared the anguish of my relationship with Debra as well as my failed marriage. Sarah walked to the fireplace. After several seconds she turned and looked me in the eyes. "Ryan, I want you to be openly honest with me about my daughters, especially Lindsey. I won't think ill of you if you feel this is something you either cannot or just don't want in your life. God blessed me with Lindsey. Even though she is a joy in my heart, there are days it can be completely overwhelming. I also know some people feel uncomfortable around children like her and I will totally understand if you feel the same. Only, Ryan, please be honest with *yourself*, because the responsibility of her care is a big consideration."

Can I dare be honest about my thoughts concerning Lindsey? I was ashamed of some of my thoughts, but Sarah wanted total honesty. I got up and started to pace, rubbing sweat from my hands. Sarah had the courage to lay her heart on the line. How could I not do the same? "I could really use a glass of wine," I said, trying to buy time. "Would you like some?"

"Sure, that would be great," she replied.

I poured our wine and returned to the living room. Sarah had put more wood on the fire and was petting Red. "I've made you uncomfortable, haven't I?" she asked. "Ryan, please don't be. I know this is a sensitive issue, and I'm not here to judge you. Please tell me how you feel."

Her sincerity gave me the courage that I couldn't find on my own. Finally, I sat next to her and bared the truth. I told her I thought the responsibility of taking care of Lindsey was an awesome one and I did feel somewhat uneasy when I was around her, and that I realized that most of this was ignorance. I told her I was scared and didn't know if I could handle a severely disabled child. "Sarah," I said, "I feel awful admitting this to you." When I turned my search for love over to God, this is not what I expected.

"Don't, don't," she insisted. "Believe me, I understand, but if you could allow yourself to get to know her, in time you'd see the delightful girl she is. You'd see she has wants and needs like any child. And don't feel sorry for her. She laughs, she experiences joy, and she is loved. She'll love you too if you give her a chance."

As I looked at Sarah I felt like I was looking at an angel, so pure in her love for this child, a child whose spastic muscles would tighten up terribly at just a touch or a loud noise. She saw a lovely child who laughed and cried like any other, who needed love and could return that love. Sarah had made me realize that if I didn't allow myself to get closer to Lindsey I would never see past her disability. Everyone always referred to me as such a nice guy. Now I wondered about that. But I knew that Sarah's kind and gentle way made me feel that everything could be okay.

"Ryan, I've shared my heart, my feelings with you. I really need to know how you feel about all this."

I nodded. "I know you do. Would you mind if we took a little break? I could use some fresh air. Come with me while I leave Red out for a little bit."

"Okay, but you can't get out of this," she said, poking my ribs.

We put on our coats and followed Red outside. It was a clear and cold night; the moon showered its glow on the new fallen snow that blanketed the grass and fields. The air felt good against my face. I put my arm around Sarah as we walked into the yard. As I stared up at the moonlit sky I wondered if I was really ready to commit to this lady I held in my arms. Was I even worthy of her love? *Lord, give me the courage to bare my heart and soul to her. I know she deserves nothing less.* I didn't want to lose her, but was I ready to commit to another relationship? On the outside, I'm sure I seemed calm, but inside I was a nervous wreck.

As we headed back to the house, I knew I'd have to relive the abuse of my childhood and the mistakes of my past, things that I'd just as soon forget. Did I dare risk the heartbreak that could also come with it? I seriously questioned whether or not I could survive another broken heart.

It was now ten-thirty. I hung our coats and poured Red some water. We refilled our wine glasses and quietly walked to the living room. I placed another couple of logs on the fire and sat down. Part of me just wanted to tell Sarah I wasn't ready for a serious relationship, but I knew that would break her heart. My insecurity and doubts were growing.

I took Sarah's hands in mine. "I'm not sure where to begin, but I'll try to be as honest with you as you've been with me. After my last relationship I took a lot of time to think and reflect. I always thought I was a loving and caring man, but I had to wonder why my relationships always failed. Was I just picking the wrong women, or was something wrong with *me?* I knew I needed some answers. My mistakes were too disappointing and painful. And the guilt I feel for my son is overwhelming sometimes." I got up and walked around the sofa.

"Go on," Sara said softly.

"Well, I discovered some things about myself. You know both my parents are deceased."

She nodded. "I believe you lost your mother when you were only eleven."

"Yes, but what I haven't told you is the horrible memories afterward. My mom and dad were separated when she died. He was seeing another woman who quickly became my stepmother. I so missed my mother and was desperate for someone to love me. My hope was my new stepmother would provide that. Well, she never did. In fact, I think she hated me. It was as if she didn't want to see me happy for a single moment. She would beat me with a cane and I could never understand why. Then my dad was in a horrible accident that left him paralyzed, and while he spent a year recuperating she became my living nightmare. I'd pray to God to allow me to be asleep when she came home so she might leave me alone, but my prayers were often ignored. She'd come in and yell at me to get up. Terrified, I wouldn't move, and soon she'd come screaming after me. She'd pull me out of bed and just start hitting me with this cane, sometimes until she drew blood.

Sarah looked at me in disbelief.

"This went on for a couple of years, until I had grown enough to fend her off. One Friday she came home late. I heard her coming up the stairs. I prayed again to let this be a night of peace, but through the door she came, yelling and screaming for me to get out of bed. I begged and pleaded, crying the whole time for her to leave me alone. The sharp crack of that cane over my back sent me to the floor, bleeding, and she kept hitting me. I ran for my bed, numb from the fear and the pain, and all I could think was, *Why, God, why are you allowing this to happen to me?* I wanted my mom back so bad. I thought, *Wait till I show Dad tomorrow. He'll take care of you.* I fell asleep finally, knowing that tomorrow he would come to my rescue.

When we arrived at the hospital, I couldn't wait for a chance to be alone with my father. Finally she left, maybe to see a doctor or get a drink. I didn't know where she had gone, nor did I care. I just knew I was alone with my dad. I pulled my pants down so he could see the cuts and bruises. He looked for a minute, then told me to pull my pants back up. Never said a word to her and never did a thing about it. I was crushed. He was my only hope to rescue me from a living hell and he did nothing." I was close to tears from the memories. I paused for a moment to regain my composure.

"Ryan," Sarah said, "she must have been a monster. how could anyone ever treat a child that way?"

"I don't know," I continued. "And I didn't know what to do or where to turn. By this time she had alienated most of our relatives, and abuse was handled a lot differently back then. They usually assumed the child was lying, at least that's what I understood. I felt hopelessly alone. Pleasing her any way I could became my plan for survival. I learned to sense her moods and would always do extra housework or wash, or anything. It brought me no happiness, but the beatings became less frequent. She continued to make my life miserable until I turned seventeen and left."

I took a deep breath, exhausted. I gulped the rest of my wine. Sarah, wiping tears from her eyes, reached over and hugged me. I was surprised how much her touch comforted me. Rubbing the wetness from around my eyes, I continued. "She took my childhood from me. I had no self-esteem. I felt lonely and worthless. Now I realize that I got married the first time because I was so insecure and afraid to be alone. Her family gave me acceptance and love, things I hadn't felt since my mother died. But when things got bad, I would resort to what kept me alive during those awful years. Soon I couldn't distinguish the line between what my feeling inspired me to *do* and what I would try to deliberately *create*. It extended the length of our marriage, but her affairs put an end to the illusion of security I had created." I wiped perspiration from my forehead. "Some of what I'm sharing with you I have shared with no one else. I'm not sure why I'm telling you, but I think it's important you know."

"Ryan, it's hard for me to express in words what it means to me for you to open yourself up like this. I know this can't be easy for you."

That's an understatement, I thought.

Sarah gently rubbed her fingers through my hair. "Do you have any idea how wonderful a man you are? How you survived all you've been through and remained a loving and compassionate man astonishes me. "It's hard for me to even relate to because my childhood was filled with fond memories and loving parents. The terrible heartache you've experienced, well, it makes me want to cry."

Her tears started to flow again. I wiped them away and told her there was no need to cry. "I hope you know I didn't tell you all this to gain your pity."

"Ryan, Ryan," she said, rubbing her hands over my cheeks. "I know that, don't even think that."

Her touch filled me with strength and comfort. A few minutes ago I was emotionally drained, but now I had a new strength to continue. "I've fallen in love with you. I was going to say so after dinner at your place and I stopped myself."

"Why?"

"Because I wasn't sure if it was real love I felt or just the start of another illusion. You deserve better than that, and that is why our relationship scares me. How do I know what I'm feeling is real? I don't want to hurt someone as special as you. God help you for falling in love with me."

"Now stop that kind of talk," she snapped back.

"And Lindsay," I said, shaking my head. "I'm not saying that I couldn't learn to love her, but right now I see a lifetime of constant care and I know that sounds shallow of me, but you asked for honesty and I'm doing my best to oblige."

"I know you are."

"You have never pressured me for my time or for a more serious relationship. Even now you're understanding and compassionate. I don't trust myself. There's baggage from the past that still haunts me and I'm afraid I'm not worthy of you." I buried my head in my hands. We sat in silence for what seemed like an eternity. When I looked up, Sarah was just watching me, not saying a word.

Finally, she spoke. "Ryan, you dumb, dumb man," she said, smiling. "You really don't have a clue, do you?"

"About what?"

"About how many women would die to have a chance to love a man like you. You act like a man with nothing to offer. I've watched you, *really* watched you. Love and kindness are who you are. I've watched you with your son. You don't develop a loving bond with a child like Brent unless you're a very loving and considerate parent. I even watched how you are with your dog. You may not realize it, but he hangs on your every word. And the one time I saw you scold him, it broke his heart. Don't you see? I wasn't looking to fall in love with you, but how could I not after being around you? If you truly believe I'm so special then believe also that you must be special for me to love you like I do."

Her words shot into my heart. Her loving aura told me that I, for this moment, was loved, truly loved, and very special. I smiled and began to cry. "I love you." She smiled and we kissed for a long, long time until I was dizzy from the storm of passion erupting between us. Finally, lightheaded from her kiss, we broke apart. I was speechless. Sarah leaned back and tried to catch her breath.

"Look," I finally said, "can we take this one day at a time, no pressure? I'll be loving and totally honest, but I can't promise anything more. Not yet. You deserve to have me whole, Sarah, not just a part of me with baggage. I don't want to wind up hurting you because I haven't dealt with my demons."

She smiled. "I won't ask for anything more."

The honesty and intimacy we shared that evening, while tough, left me with feelings of hope. "I do love you, Sarah."

"I love you, too."

CHAPTER SIX

The next several weeks were hectic. There were Christmas pageants at school along with the normal bustle of preparing for my favorite holiday, and then a week before Christmas we got six inches of snow, adding to the festive spirit. Brent was excited by Santa's impending arrival. Sarah and I took all the kids to see him and leave their lists. If they had any doubts in Old Saint Nick, they didn't let on. Lindsey wasn't much impressed, but she loved being pushed through the mall in her wheelchair. She laughed and giggled at the bustle of the shoppers and screamed her excitement when we stopped to eat. Brent and Elisha on the other hand were totally caught up in the holiday excitement.

Though my time with Lindsey had been limited, I was beginning to understand what Sarah had told me. Though she didn't talk she had her own way of communicating. When she was content or in agreement, she would take the back of her right hand and rub it back across her right cheek. And she had this little cough she would make when she wanted to be part of the conversation. Some people would look and stare, and I would feel a little uneasy, but I was improving. As for Sarah, she paid no attention to the stares and comments, her Lindsey was as precious as any other child there. As I observed Sarah in these situations, my admiration for her grew. Elisha was like her mother, her sister was special. I noticed Brent was still somewhat uneasy around Lindsey. We both had some growing to do, but we were trying. Sarah was a natural around the children and opened her heart to my son immediately. I breathed a sigh of hope. maybe it was possible for another woman to truly love and accept my child. Whether she knew it or not, Sarah was slowly helping me regain my faith in women.

Brent and I got our tree on Saturday afternoon. It was a tradition for us to go out and cut our own tree. We didn't usually wait this late, but somehow the time had crept up on us. It didn't matter because we always had a wonderful time. "Hey, Dad, how about this one?" he shouted, pointing to the tree towering over him.

I laughed. It had to be eleven or twelve feet tall. "Uh, I think it may be a little too big," I said.

"Oh, I guess you're right." He quickly ran to another. We finally picked one we thought was just right. We cut it down and, together, we dragged it to the truck, singing "Jingle Bells" along the way. Jeb Snyder, the owner of the tree farm, recognized us as we stopped to pay for the tree.

"You picked a darn nice tree, Brent," he said, patting Brent's head. "How you two doing?"

"Oh, we're fine. We always enjoy coming here," I replied.

"Yeah, it's fun!" Brent chimed in.

We wished Jeb a merry Christmas and headed home. I loved making Christmas a special time for Brent. Most of my Christmases were unhappy. Dad never put up a real tree or shared in the festivities. And after my stepmother entered the picture they became holidays that I was better off not remembering at all.

Once home, we cut the tree to size and put in the stand. The smell of pine in the living room filled our senses and I smiled in appreciation for the blessings we shared. We decorated the tree while drinking eggnog and eating our own home-baked cookies. Christmas carols filled the house and we laughed and sang along with them. Brent always enjoyed putting the angel on top of the tree. "She's pretty, don't you think?" he'd always say. When we finished, we'd both stand back and proudly admire our tree. Red always loved the cookies and he'd beg until we finally gave in. His enthusiastic tail-wagging appreciation usually knocked a few ornaments off the tree.

We finally sat back on the couch, exhausted from the day's activities. I put my arm around Brent. "You know," I said, "We sure are good tree decorators."

"We sure are," came his reply.

With just the lights from the tree and the glow from the fireplace, we sat back filled with the joy of the season as Eddy Arnold sang "Silent Night." I squeezed my arm around my son drawing him next to me, my heart filled with love and gratitude for these special moments we shared together.

The next five days seemed to fly by with office Christmas parties and last-minute shopping. The weather had turned cold with snow predicted for Christmas Eve. I always took two weeks off for the holiday season, so I had time to really enjoy this wonderful time of year with family and friends, especially with my son.

Christmas Eve was on Thursday. Sarah and I decided to take Elisha and Brent to Christmas Eve service. Sarah's parents agreed to watch Lindsey. They were terrific people who welcomed me into their family with open arms.

We headed for church as a light snow began to fall. Elisha and Brent screamed with excitement, sharing their impatience for Christmas morning to arrive. We sang carols and laughed as we drove to church. The evening was total joy. I parked the car and Brent and Elisha jumped out, tilting their heads back to catch snowflakes on their tongues. Sarah and I joined them, inviting their laughter. I guess adults look funny catching snowflakes on their tongues. As we walked up the steps, music from the church organ filled the air. Sarah and I, arm in arm with Brent and Elisha in front, walked to our seats.

Reverend William Kern presided over the service. He was a rather young man of the cloth, but his personable nature and youthful enthusiasm for his love of God made his sermons a joy to listen to. They were beautiful and moving.

Looking around at the overflowing pews, people awash in God's love, I wondered why we couldn't carry this spirit throughout the year. How beautiful the world would be and how differently our children would grow if we kept moments like this in the forefront of our lives instead of allowing them to fade into day-to-day chaos. After the service ended, everyone wished each other a merry Christmas. We walked outside and witnessed God's beauty. He had painted the town in several inches of pure white snow. Children ran and laughed along with their parents. Sarah and I smiled at each other as we chased after Elisha and Brent.

On the way home they pleaded with us to let them open one gift. We pretended to be deep in thought which prompted more begging and pleading. Unable to hold back our laughter any longer, we finally agreed, to their loud cheers.

When we arrived at Sarah's her parents greeted us at the door. Elisha announced loudly, "We get to open one gift. Mom said so." They laughed as her grandpa picked her up and gave her a hug.

"What makes you think there are any gifts for you, anyway?" Elisha's grandpa said teasingly. "Santa hasn't made his rounds yet."

"Mom always gives me a gift on Christmas Eve because I'm a good girl," she said.

Sarah brought in two packages to their gleeful screams. Elisha opened a board game and Brent a model airplane. "Can we play, can we play?" Elisha asked, full of excitement.

"Oh, I guess for a little while if it's okay with Ryan."

Elisha ran over and jumped in my lap. "Please, please," she pleaded. How could I even think of any answer but yes? She gave me a big hug and scurried off to her room, Brent on her heels.

Sarah's parents said they had to be going and wished us a merry Christmas. "Now you know you're invited for dinner tomorrow, Ryan," Sarah's mom said.

"I'll be there."

"Please drive careful," Sarah said as they headed out.

We stood at the door, watching them leave. The snow had slowed, but still had turned the night into a winter wonderland. Sarah leaned back against me, snuggling her head against my neck. "Isn't it simply beautiful?"

"Yes, it is." We stood there, Sarah in my arms, drinking in the specialness of the evening.

She closed the door, turned around, and kissed me. "I love you, Ryan. Thanks for spending Christmas Eve with us."

She walked into the kitchen, then turned around with a devilish look on her face. "What?" I asked.

"Oh, I'm just thinking about the presents I bought you. I hope you like them. I'm so excited, I can hardly wait to see you open them!"

"But it's not Christmas," I gently protested.

"Oh, please, just one."

"Okay," I said, "There's one I wanted to give you this evening, too." I went out to the car, enjoying the fresh-fallen snow. My mind raced back to when I was little and Christmas snows were a regular occurrence. I thought about my mother and I looked to the heavens. "Merry Christmas, Mom. I really miss you." I thought about how much pleasure she would have gotten from her grandson. I felt a great sense of loss as I slowly walked back to the house.

Sarah had put on some hot chocolate for the kids who were now watching *The Night Before Christmas*.

We sat in the living room. Sarah gave me a box wrapped in red paper with silver ribbon. I thought, *a shirt or a sweater*. I gave her mine. "You go first," she insisted.

"I know what it is," Elisha said. "But I can't tell"

I gently pulled off the wrapping paper and opened the box. After taking out layers of tissue, I finally uncovered her gift. A rush of emotions washed over me, and I struggled to hold back my tears.

"What's wrong, Mom?" Elisha asked, confused by my reaction.

I looked up from the box to see everyone staring at me. "It's all right, Elisha," I said, wiping the tears from my face.

"Do you like it?" she asked.

Regaining my composure, I told her it was one of the most wonderful gifts I had ever received. She smiled. "What is it?" Brent asked.

"It's a picture of your grandmother," I said, as he stood next to me. "Sarah, how? How did you do this?"

"I remembered you telling me how you only had a single snapshot of your mother. So I asked your brother if he had one, and he gave it to me. The photo place in town made a copy and enlarged it."

There, in a beautiful eight-by-ten frame, was the largest portrait of my mother I had ever owned. "She was a beautiful woman, Ryan," Sarah said softly.

"She's really pretty, Dad," Brent added.

"It's funny, I was just thinking about her when I went to the car. I don't know how to thank you, Sarah. And you too, Elisha." I gave them both a kiss and a hug and then excused myself. I went to the bathroom and closed the door and allowed the emotions to freely pour out. Joy and sadness, gratitude and loss, all mixed together. After several minutes, I washed my face with cold water and rejoined the group. Sarah gave me a loving glance as I sat down. I thanked her again and presented her with her gift.

She opened the box and gasped, putting her hand to her chest. She gently pulled the necklace from its case. "Ryan, it's gorgeous! you shouldn't have," she said.

"Brent helped me pick it out."

"Well, thank you both, you certainly have good taste." We all laughed as I clumsily helped her put it on. "Thanks, Ryan," she said, leaning over to give me a kiss. "I'll cherish this always."

Together we finished watching *The Night Before Christmas*. When the movie ended, I told Sarah we had to be going. As I leaned down to give Elisha a hug, she wrapped her arms around my neck and whispered in my ear, "Are you going to marry my mommy?" This question, coming from a child, would have made me cringe at any other time in my life. Now all I could do was smile.

"I don't know, honey," I said as I patted her shoulder

"What did she say?" Sarah asked.

"Oh, nothing," I said, giving Elisha a quick wink. "It's a secret."

It was close to midnight. Brent ran to the car, playing in the snow along the way. I expressed my thanks to Sarah for the wonderful evening and the precious gift she had given me.

"I'll help you hang her picture," she said.

We kissed and wished each other a merry Christmas. "I'll see you tomorrow!" I called as I walked to the
car.

CHAPTER SEVEN

Christmas day went off with the normal seasonal fanfare. Brent and I opened gifts in the morning along with Red. Then we stopped at Sarah's to finish our gift giving before taking Brent to his mom's to stay until the following evening.

Then I drove Sarah and her daughters to her parents for Christmas dinner. I met many of Sarah's relatives. They made me feel genuinely welcome and all seemed like very nice people. Her father played Santa, which was no stretch at all. He was born to play the part, with white hair and beard, and a pot belly to boot. He was a natural.

We loaded the presents in the car and I invited Sarah over to my place for the evening.

As we drove the twenty miles back to my house, Sarah filled me in on her family. Her brother, John, was a machinist and a Harley enthusiast, along with his wife, Sue, and two children. Her nephew, Mike, had just gotten his wings as a fighter pilot for the Navy. Her sister, Mary, was in cosmetics and a real go-getter. Uncle Jake was the colorful relative with the effervescent personality. He could sell you swamp land in Florida and make you think he was doing you a favor. "Oh, by the way," Sarah asked, "what did my daughter whisper in your ear last night?"

"What did she tell you?"

"She just giggles when I ask her."

"Well, I guess it's okay to tell you," I said. "She wanted to know if I was going to marry her mommy."

"What?" Sarah screamed. "You're kidding!"

"No, I'm serious. In fact, I wondered if you had put her up to it. Just teasing," I quickly added.

"I just can't believe she asked you that."

"Why? I'm a pretty good catch," I said, laughing.

"You remember what I told you about how she feels about men. This is really out of character for her. And you wonder why I say I think you're possessed. You even have my daughter under your spell."

I looked over at her with raised eyebrows.

"Ryan, I'm serious. What kind of power do you have over us?"

"Oh, I'll never tell," I said. We pulled in the driveway and Red cheerfully greeted us at the door before running off in the snow. He soon returned, snow covering his head and back. I told him to shake it off and we went inside. Sarah volunteered to make coffee while I built a fire. Red had grown accustomed to Sarah buying him snacks, and I could hear him begging in the kitchen. "And you said I was possessed. Look what you've done to my dog," I said.

After I got the fire going, I joined Sarah in the kitchen. She poured our coffee and we sat at the table to exchange stories of Christmas morning and the excitement of watching the children open their gifts. "You know, Sarah, after I divorced, I was really apprehensive that first Christmas. It was just Brent and me, and though we both enjoyed the holiday season, I wondered what Christmas morning would be like. How would Brent react without his mom being there? But it was the best Christmas I have ever experienced. Instead of the usual distractions, I just sat back and watched him open every present.

All the joy I felt was in sharing his excitement with every package he opened. And I think Brent truly enjoyed being in sole possession of my attention. I'll never forget it."

"I think I had some of the same reservations," Sarah said, "but their father never really got into Christmas unless he was trying to impress someone. I can remember one Christmas Eve he went out to be with one of his girlfriends and didn't come home until four-thirty in the morning. I vowed that would be the last Christmas we would spend together. It was so nice, our first Christmas by ourselves." Sarah said, looking back. "The girls and I just left our hearts open to the joy of the holidays. It was such a relief not to have their father's abusive behavior cloud the holidays." She smiled at me

"We've both come a long way," I said.

We finished our coffee and Sarah suggested we find the perfect place to hang my mother's picture. We finally decided the living room was the ideal location. After the picture was hung, I stood back to appreciate the visual presence of my mother. I thanked Sarah again. We decided to watch *It's a Wonderful Life* since it was a holiday tradition for Sarah. "You know," I said, "I don't believe I've ever seen this movie the whole way through."

"You're kidding!"

"No, I'm serious."

"Oh, you don't know what you've been missing," she replied. "This is going to be a treat for you. Oh, and I just love Jimmy Stewart."

"Oh, you do?"

"Yes, he's a great actor, but even more so because he's a true family man." As the movie started, Sarah snuggled close on the couch. Being the sentimental fool I am, I fell in love with the story and its message. How could you not feel moved and inspired as good conquered evil and generosity won over greed?

And to my surprise, God, in his creative genius, gave me an answer to a question I had asked myself in those tough times. George's angel, Clarence, showed him how much of a difference his life made to others, how his caring and compassion rippled through an entire town.

I could remember, in my darkest days, wondering what difference it would make if I were gone, how much better off my loved ones would be if I were out of the way. God's message struck me loud and clear. We are all special, we are all his miracles, and we can never know the endless lives we touch by our example.

Of course, Sarah and I both had wet eyes by the end of the movie. "Wasn't that good?" she asked. "Did you enjoy it?"

I assured her I did. "That's my kind of movie, too," I said. "And to think I've been missing it all these years."

I poured us some Baileys over ice and came back to the living room. We sipped our drinks and enjoyed the warmth of the fire. Sarah put her drink down and looked at me intently. "Ryan, do you mind if I tell you something?"

"No," I replied. "What would you like to tell me?"

"The past couple of months have been very special and dear to me. You and your son have brought real joy into our lives. You've opened your heart to my girls. I just can't thank you enough. Oh, and thanks for ruining me too!"

"Ruining you? How?"

"Before, I was content, and now all I can think about is you. When we're apart I ache, like a piece of me is missing. I think we've found something very special. Tell me you feel it, too," she said, almost pleading.

"I do, Sarah," I said, bringing her closer to me. "I love you, and though part of me wants to deny it, I can't. You have showed me what real love is and I trust you, I mean *really* trust you. This is a huge step for me, because I wondered if I would ever truly trust another woman again."

As we kissed, the intensity between us grew. I took her hand and led her upstairs, our level of intimacy and desire deeply profound, almost like an out-of-body experience. There was something very different about making love with Sarah. Every touch, each caress, filled with such passion and intensity, like currents of electricity arcing between us. The depth of the feeling between us was like unspoken words, our expression of love reaching the very depths of our beings.

I realized for the first time that making love is not about sex at all. Sex, good or bad, can leave one feeling shallow and empty, while the love and complete satisfaction I felt with Sarah became a permanent thread that wove through and strengthened the fabric of our bond.

We laid in each other's arms, talking far into the night, sharing our hopes and our dreams. As I felt her soft, milky skin against mine, I realized that maybe God had answered my prayers. Here lying next to me was my soul mate, my missing half, the love of my life. We fell off to sleep holding each other close, our hearts beating together.

CHAPTER EIGHT

As the months passed our love continued to blossom. I felt whole and alive, and I knew that my heart had been freed and the love that flowed forth was pure and natural. I was the happiest I ever felt in my life, but my demons and my insecurities still lurked in the shadows. What if this didn't last? Slowly, Lindsey and I grew closer. The more I was around her, the more I knew how to relate to this dear girl. Sarah would joyfully watch us interact. She was a witness to the growth I was experiencing.

Though we still lived in our separate homes, we were bonding, truly bonding as a family. Sarah was nurturing and gentle, but firm. Our parenting philosophies were almost identical. And we knew that they had to be if we were to ever evolve into a real family. We knew in time our children would eventually try to play us against each another. It would only be natural.

With the coming of spring our love continued to flourish and grow. We spent more time together, especially with the children. Elisha would ask now and then if we were going to get married. That still made me nervous. Apparently, this step was still an obstacle to be overcome. We only ever discussed it briefly, despite our deep, true love, and we realized we both felt the same way. After all the pain and heartache of prior relationships, we were content with how things were. Everything was going so well, why risk bringing marriage into it? We discussed the possibility of moving in together and I was much more relaxed with that. Sarah was not. She felt strongly that for us to become a family, we had to be a married couple. So for now things would stay as they were.

With the warm weather, outside activity was on the increase—lawns being fertilized, gardens being tilled, farmers planting their fields, and birds building their nests.

Sarah and I both loved the outdoors. I always loved planting a vegetable garden and flowers. Like a child, I was in awe of God's beautiful creation and was thankful for it. Working in the soil and nurturing plants to their fullness, well, I found it to be both relaxing and therapeutic. It was easy for me to leave my troubles, let my problems slip away as my fingers worked the soil. The satisfaction and the miracle of nurturing seeds into a beautiful garden bursting with abundance, or watching a flowerbed evolve into an endless procession of colors and shapes, never ceased to amaze me.

One afternoon Sarah stopped by to help. I felt so blessed that we shared the same labor of love. We planted rows of seeds and seedlings of peppers, tomatoes, and other vegetables. We talked over our plans, our hopes, and our dreams under the warmth of the spring sun. Working in the dirt, the sweat pouring off of us, was sheer enjoyment.

I looked up and found Sarah staring at me. "What?" I asked.

"Oh, nothing. I'm just watching you."

"Why?"

"Just witnessing another one of your wonderful qualities."

"What, digging in the dirt?"

"Yes. I've watched how gentle you are when you put each plant in the soil."

I gave her a dazed look, but smiled.

"Ryan, I'm serious, and don't laugh."

"Okay," I said, "but this is how I do it."

"I know, you water each plant and then pat the dirt around it with so much care. While I enjoy gardening, I have to confess, I'm not very successful. You, on the other hand, have quite the green thumb."

I kindly shrugged off her remarks.

"Ryan," she said, "Let's take a break. Come and sit next to me."

I brushed my hands off, wiped the sweat from my forehead, and joined her.

"I think you're making light of what I'm saying," she said.

"I don't mean to," I replied, kissing her cheek.

"You still don't realize what a wonderful man you are." I sat there giving her my attention. I didn't understand the connection with my gardening techniques. "I love you so much because of the special man you are. Remember you saying how much you used to observe my actions in the beginning because you were filled with distrust? Well, I notice little things about you, too, and not out of distrust, but out of my ever-growing love. I watch you with the children, with Red, with other people—how kind and loving you are, how everyone you meet or have come into your home, how you make them feel they're special. And yes, even watching you plant your garden. Your caring and gentleness come through your hands and your fingers as you plant each flower and vegetable. When you wonder why I love you like I do, it's because of the special man you are. And that's why I get so upset when you put yourself down the way you do sometimes. I just don't think you truly appreciate the wonderful gifts that God has given you."

I leaned back, my arms stretched behind me, and just watched her. Her kind words touched me. She sat with her legs to one side, her hands in flowered gloves, and her long auburn hair flowing from beneath her straw hat, her face speckled with dirt. Oh, she was a gorgeous sight, radiating beauty, taking my breath away. I fell in love with her all over again.

I reached over and wiped the dirt from her cheek. "I love you, Sarah. Sometimes I can't say it enough." I pulled her with me as I stood and she wrapped her arms around my neck.

"And I so love you, Ryan." Elisha and Brent came running from the trampoline in the side yard and joined our hugging. Red, feeling left out, ran up and jumped on us, making us lose our balance and fall to the ground. We all roared with laughter.

If I we're going to marry again, here was the woman I would risk trying with. But my demons of the past still hadn't released their hold on me. Everything was fine and good, but I knew that, as long as we weren't married, I still had a way out. All the wonderful things Sarah had brought into my life, and I was still afraid of a lifelong commitment. Was I being wise and cautions thinking like this? Or was I just plain stupid?

I knew one thing for sure: I needed to resolve these inner issues before I could take the next step in our relationship. But did I dare share these feelings with Sarah? I didn't have a choice. I knew I had to be honest with her.

CHAPTER NINE

Over the next several weeks Sarah seemed in an extraordinarily jovial mood. I thought maybe the summer season had brought out her spirited exuberance. Happiness and joy had settled into our lives. Over the past nine months, we had fallen deeply in love. Yes, we went from wanting no relationship to riding the soaring wings of love. Oh, what a powerful force when it strikes!

Sarah had been terrific from the very first meeting. She was loving and kind and patient. For the first time since my mother had passed away, I felt loved purely for the person I was. But my doubts, my insecurities, the scars from a lifetime of tragedy and turmoil still had their hold on me. And when they would surface it would have an impact on our relationship. I could sense Sarah was becoming somewhat impatient that we weren't moving closer toward marriage. While Sarah was very understanding of what I was dealing with, I knew her understanding had its limits. There was certainly an urgency for me to resolve my issues. But how? I was so afraid of the permanence in our relationship. I mean, here I was, in love with a wonderfully magnificent lady, and part of me was paralyzed with fear. I knew deep down that I would have to eventually understand and rid myself of this plague or risk losing the woman of my dreams.

So, when Sarah suggested a long weekend getaway to the shore, just the two of us, I thought it was a wonderful idea. I didn't know why I thought getting away would bring forth any answers, but I knew we had to have a heart-to-heart talk. I couldn't keep these feelings buried inside any longer, especially since I sensed Sarah's desire to move forward. I would just play it by ear.

We decided to leave the following Friday since I was scheduled for Lasik eye surgery the following week. Sarah made the reservations. I could hear the excitement in her voice as she shared with me where we were staying.

As I drove to Sarah's early Friday morning, I was anxious to get going. We had made arrangements for the children and Red. It would be nice to get away. Sarah cheerfully greeted me at the door, wrapped her arms around me, and gave me a kiss. "Good morning," she said. Her bags were packed and ready by the front door. As she walked through her house checking everything one last time, she yelled from the kitchen, "I'm so looking forward to this trip."

I shouted back, "Me too!" and took her bags to the car. The sun was already up and there was a warm breeze. It was a great day to be alive.

Sarah locked the front door, and I put my arm around her as we walked to the car. I turned the key, leaned over, and gave her a kiss. She smiled and motioned for me to drive. I laughed. I had packed some of our favorite CDs and Sarah brought refreshments.

We thoroughly loved being together, and the road slipped by with ease. We had about a four-hour drive ahead of us. Traffic was light, and we made great time. We laughed and sang as the miles clipped by.

We talked about the kids and how well they were doing in school and how truly blessed we were to have such wonderful children. Our conversation effortlessly drifted from one topic to another. Sarah was radiant; she never looked more beautiful, but there was something different about her, too, or so I thought. I dismissed it as just a symptom of my excitement over our getaway.

After taking a few detours to do some antique shopping, we arrived in Ocean City around one-thirty. The condo Sarah reserved was on the bay side. As I turned into the parking lot, I voiced my approval of her choice. Soft pastel colors decorated the exterior stucco and meticulously kept gardens surrounded the property and pool. The lobby was plush and luxurious with a beautiful fountain dancing in its center. Luscious green plants and flowers were everywhere. I looked at Sarah. "Nothing too good for you, honey," she said. She always made me feel special.

We walked out to the car to retrieve our luggage. The sun was warm and the fragrance of the ocean filled the air. In mock dancing, I twirled Sarah around in the parking lot until she fell into my arms. "I love you, Ryan," she said softly, her eyes meeting mine.

"I love you, too."

"Come on, hurry," she said. "I want to see our room." We grabbed our luggage and ran to our condo.

It was beautifully decorated and furnished with all the amenities of the shore. We stepped out onto the balcony. The vastness of the bay stretched for miles before us. Seagulls danced in the air currents just a few feet away. "Part of our welcoming committee," I joked. Below us a couple dug for clams. To our left we heard music and screams of delight from the pool. Off in the distance sailboats lazily floated on the water. "Oh, how I love the shore, Ryan," Sarah said, snuggling close to me. Our love radiated between us. "Thank you for agreeing to come," she said, looking up at me. "I so love you, Ryan, and I'm so thankful for the joy you brought into my life." I leaned down and gently kissed her lips.

We decided to eat at Norma's Seafood House, described as having the best seafood in town and was owned by the same family for over forty years. Nestled right on the bay, it was within walking distance from where we were staying.

We requested a window table overlooking the bay so we could enjoy the sunset. We ordered a bottle of Merlot, and an appetizer platter with steamed clams and mussels. For our entree, we both decided on lobster. We toasted our first night at the shore together and enjoyed a romantic dinner. The sunset was spectacular, a huge red ball resting on the horizon. As we sipped after-dinner coffee, the huge sun slowly slipped away, painting the sky in brilliant shades of red and purple. We held hands, peered deeply into each other's eyes, and lost ourselves in the moment.

Once we came back to reality, we paid our check and slowly walked back to our room. The town was bustling and a soft breeze kissed our faces as we walked. "Ryan," Sarah said, squeezing my hand, "tell me this will never end."

"What's that?"

"Us. Everything with you is so special. Everything. I pray to God it never will end."

"Well, since we keep saying God brought us together, I think we're on pretty stable ground, don't you?"

She leaned up and kissed my cheek. "Yes, I think we are," she said as she wrapped her arm around mine. "Yes, we are," I heard her whisper again.

When we got back to our room, we crashed on the bed. We were both exhausted from the trip. Holding her in my arms, we quickly fell off to sleep.

The next morning I awoke to the calls of seagulls and the roaring of boat motors as crabbers and fishermen headed out for the day's catches. The sun was barely up. I slipped out of bed and walked to the balcony.

One boat after another left its dock and headed out to sea. A few couples were already up taking their morning strolls. I walked back into the bedroom and sat on the edge of the bed. Sarah looked so content and peaceful as she slept. And, yes, she looked beautiful, too. And though I teased her about her natural beauty in the morning, she really was. Little did I know that before this weekend was over, I would shatter her peace and dreams.

CHAPTER TEN

I kissed Sarah's cheek as she stirred awake. "Oh, good morning, honey," she said somewhat groggily.

"Good morning," I said. "It's going to be another beautiful day." I laid back down beside her and she rolled into my arms.

"Mmmm, that's better," she sighed.

After all this time I still couldn't get over the feeling of wonder and sensuality and intimacy I felt whenever we were next to one another. Just holding her was deeply satisfying.

We finally got up and showered and headed out for breakfast. Afterward we took a nice walk on the beach. We enjoyed the simple beauty of nature, of God's wondrous creations. I had learned early on in life that the simple things were the true treasures to be appreciated.

"Ryan, do you mind if we come back to the beach this evening?" Sarah asked.

"Why, no. Why?"

"Oh, I think it will be purely divine with the full moon and you. It will be perfect."

"What will?" I asked.

"Oh, nothing."

We spent the rest of the morning visiting stores and doing some shopping. In the afternoon we sunbathed on the beach, sipping drinks and relaxing. We were having a wonderful time.

We decided to eat at one of the pubs on the boardwalk. Sarah looked simply ravishing in her white sleeveless sundress, her beautiful auburn hair draped softly over her shoulders. "You look beautiful this evening," I said, as we walked the boards.

"And you look very handsome, sir, and sexy," she replied. The boardwalk was filling with people as darkness settled upon us.

We came upon an Irish pub with tables outside along the boardwalk. The hostess led us to the last empty table. "Divine intervention," Sarah joked. We ordered drinks and decided to order our food a little later. It was entertaining to sit and people watch, especially at the shore. You never know what you may see.

The full moon was high in the night sky when we finished eating. We walked back to the car to get a blanket to take out on the beach. We were like two school kids in love, totally content in each other's company, walking hand-in-hand, just out of reach of the incoming waves. Once we misjudged and a wave scurried over our feet, its cold water making Sarah shriek in surprise. I couldn't help but laugh and she soon joined in. After walking for a while, we stopped to look out over the water. The moon's rays sparkled across the water in shimmering brilliance. It was stunning.

I spread our blanket on the sand. We sat down, Sarah next to me, snuggling close, leaning her head against my chest. The sound of the crashing waves lulled us into a near meditative state. Here we sat, in love, and all seemed right with the world.

"I don't know if I've ever witnessed a more beautiful night," Sarah said. "In fact, it's a perfect setting for something I want to share with you."

"I knew something was up. From the moment we left your house I sensed something."

"Oh, you did? Well, there's nothing like keeping a man in suspense, is there?"

She looked at me and smiled. We sat for several more minutes just looking out over the water. I could tell she was thinking about how to start, so I didn't interrupt the silence. She inched around on the blanket until she was facing me. Her look was serious. "Ryan, you know we love each other very much, and I think we have found something very, very special. I certainly never thought I would find true love, and until you came into my life I didn't even know what it was. I can remember reading love stories and believing deep in my heart that true love was sheer fantasy. So I convinced myself I could be happy without it. And I was, until you came along and changed everything."

"I didn't mean to."

She put her finger to my lips. "I know you didn't. You tugged at my heart where no one ever touched before. Remember all the times I accused you of being possessed? Well, I just couldn't control my feelings when it came to you. I had gotten so good at keeping my heart closed until you turned my world upside down. You scared the hell out of me, and in some ways you still do."

She was silent for a moment, her emotions starting to break through. "Your love has pierced the deepest recesses of my soul. You have awakened in me feelings so strong, so totally enveloping, that it shakes me to my core. You, Ryan, are the sparkle in my eyes, the bounce in my steps, the joy in my laughter. It scares me because I don't know what I would do if I were to ever lose you." Tears started to slowly trickle down her face. I gently squeezed her hands in mine and smiled. "Damn you. Just look what you've done to me." She forced a smile. "I love you so much and I didn't want to."

"But why?" I finally said. "I'm just not that special."

"Oh, you're such a dumb, dumb man." She started to laugh. "You are the kindest, most generous and loving man I have ever known, and you still don't realize how special and unique you are."

I was dumbfounded, bathing in the love and praise she showered upon me. I didn't feel special or unique. How could I when the shackles of the past imprisoned me so? The pain and loneliness of being unloved and unwanted and of having no worth still strangled the essence of the man I had become. The total agony of that hurt, of that pain, was as real and as strong as if it were yesterday.

"Ryan, Ryan, Ryan," Sarah said, tapping her fingers on my cheek. "Where did you go?"

"Nowhere," I said as I snapped back to reality. I realized how sad I suddenly felt.

"Did I say something wrong?"

"No, no, nothing you said," as I pulled her close. I quickly regained my composure for her sake, forced a smile, and told her to continue. She was hesitant, but I persisted.

She continued. "I'm not sure how you'll react to what I'm going to say, so, oh God, how do I do this. Ryan, I've never done anything like this before, and now I feel so awkward. I've been rehearsing this in my mind for over a week. You know," she continued, touching my hand, "how we talked about the possibility of moving in together?" I nodded. "And I feel we need to be married for that to happen. Well, after much thought . . . and here comes the scary part."

"Go ahead."

"Well . . ." She hesitated. "I would really like us to make plans to get married soon. It would make me so happy," she said, smiling. Her eyes searched mine for my reaction. "What do you think?"

I was blindsided, overwhelmed by my anxieties. I tried to find the right words. I loved Sarah very much and didn't want to say anything that would hurt her. Part of me wanted to grab her and say, *Let's do it!* but deep down I was drowning in fears of marriage and life-long commitment.

Sarah noticed the change. "You don't feel the same way, do you?"

"Yes, I do. I love you so much, but God, the talk of marriage—I don't know what comes over me when we discuss it. I don't know how to explain it to you," I said, frustrated. Tears started to roll down her face. My heart broke knowing, right at this moment, I couldn't tell her what she wanted to hear. "Sarah, don't doubt my love for you, and if I were to marry again, it would be to you, but how can I say yes when right now, inside, I'm unraveling at the seriousness of what you propose? How do I make you understand when I don't understand myself?"

I stood up and stared into the endless sea before me. The beauty had disappeared. I needed to explain myself. "Sarah, I can't until . . ." I heard her tears come flooding out. I turned and saw her running away. "Sarah!" I cried after her. "Wait, wait! You didn't let me finish!" I started to chase after her and stopped. "What's wrong with me?" I shouted, looking up to the heavens. "Damn it, what's wrong with me?" I fell to my knees in the sand, burying my face in my hands. My heart ached at what I had just done to the woman I loved. My insides were churning. "Dear God," I pleaded. "What kind of coward, what kind of man am I? What am I afraid of? Lord, please help me. Please help me." I hated myself and I certainly didn't feel special. I knew I had to go find Sarah and try to explain the mess I was inside. Maybe love doesn't conquer all.

I picked up our blanket and slowly followed after Sarah.

I spied a silhouette of a woman off in the distance sitting atop a dune. I walked toward her wondering if I could ever undo the heartache and disappointment I had just caused.

She was still sobbing. "Sarah, I'm truly sorry."

"Why, Ryan, when things are going so well between us? Why?" To see her like this saddened me to the depths of my soul, for I did love her with all of my heart. "I wanted this weekend to be so special," she said, wiping her face. Then, her eyes filled with hurt and sadness, she looked up at me. "Why doesn't all my love for you heal your pain? I wanted it to so much."

"I do love you. Please don't ever doubt that. Please," I said. "I love you more than life itself. I have a problem, and I don't know what it is, but I know before I can marry you I have to resolve it if I'm ever to be at peace. Can you be patient with me? I know this isn't fair to you." We sat a while in silence. Then I pulled her close to me, rocking back and forth, my lips resting on her hair. I whispered, "Please know how much I love you."

"I do," she whispered back. "I do."

Those two little words meant all the world to me at that moment. I made a vow to myself to resolve what troubled my soul no matter what it took. I took a deep breath and sighed from sheer emotional exhaustion.

When we got back to our room, Sarah got ready for bed. She said goodnight and kissed my forehead. I walked out to the balcony, closing the sliding door behind me. *What kind of a jerk am I?* How I hated myself. I spent the next several hours replaying the evening in my mind. What kind of coward was I? The more haunting question I had to answer was, *What kind of man am I, really?* After tonight, I wasn't sure.

CHAPTER ELEVEN

Morning came with very little sleep. It was going to be a long ride home. Sarah and I were truly in unfamiliar territory. Over the year we had been together we hadn't even had a real argument. And even this morning there was no hatefulness or bitterness, but things were definitely different. An eerie awkwardness had settled upon us.

I was still very much upset with myself for hurting her. I was reeling from the power of my fears and insecurities. I had totally underestimated how real they still were.

We tried to act cheerful on the drive home, but much of the trip was filled with miles of silence. Could I undo what I had done? I mean, this wonderful woman finally opened her heart to a man, me, and all I could do was choke on my fears. My cowardice had tarnished our fairytale romance.

I carried her bags into her house. At her front door I held her in my arms. "Sarah," I said, "Can you ever forgive me for ruining the weekend?"

She gently kissed me. "You're forgiven," she said.

"Please be patient with me. "I'll get this figured out."

As I drove home, the sadness overwhelmed me. The thought of losing her scared me. *How long can she be patient? How long?*

The rest of the day passed in a daze. The joy and happiness of the past months were gone. My sadness turned to despair, my despair into depression. I was thankful that Brent was at his mother's for the summer. I sorely missed the little guy, but I needed to be alone. I now realized that Sarah's love alone could not rid me of my fears, my insecurities, of a life-long commitment. But where would I find the answers? Over the years I had read countless books, seen a psychologist, talked to close, dear friends only to find temporary solutions. What was I missing? Was my situation hopeless?

Morning brought no answers to my questions. In fact, the more I thought about it, the more questions I asked. I spent the morning asking God for guidance.

Maybe because I was still exhausted from our trip, or too depressed to concentrate, no answers came.

That evening the phone rang. It was my best friend, Steve. "So, buddy, how was your romantic getaway?"

"Well, it started out terrific and ended in disaster."

"Why, what happened?"

"I'm not sure what to tell you except I'm screwed up."

"What do you mean, you're screwed up? Everything was going so well with you and Sarah. I thought we'd hear wedding bells soon."

"Well, I think Sarah did, too." I replied. "Steve, I blew it. She mentioned marriage and I don't know. I guess I panicked."

"Well, is everything going to be all right? Is there anything I can do?"

"Just keep being my friend. Sometimes I feel like I just need to get away by myself and concentrate on working these problems out. It would be unfair for me to think of marrying Sarah when I'm still like this."

"Are you serious about getting away?"

"I'm not sure of anything right now," I answered. "Why?"

"I was just thinking, my grandfather owns a cabin in Montana that isn't being used right now. You always said you wanted to go there. I could check with him."

"Thanks. I'll think about it. Oh, by the way, I just remembered you said you had off Friday."

"Yeah, that's right. Why?"

"I need a lift," I said. "I'm having some tests done for my Lasik surgery at two o'clock on Friday with my eye surgeon and he said they'd be putting drops in my eyes and I wouldn't be able to drive."

"I'll pick you up then," he said.

"Fine. And thanks again. I'll talk to you then."

I stopped by Sarah's on Thursday evening. She met me at the door, giving me a kiss and a hug. "How are you?" I asked.

"I'm fine," she said. "How are you?"

"I'm a mess."

"I want to help you if I can."

"Sarah," I said, "I don't know if anyone can help me. Nothing I've tried has worked. Maybe I'm crazy."

"You are not."

"Sometimes I feel as if I need to just get away by myself, away from everything."

"Well, maybe that's a good idea, somewhere you can truly get in touch with your inner self," Sarah said. "Somewhere in the middle of nowhere where it's you, nature, and God." She paused for a moment. "Ask God to help you, Ryan."

"I have."

"No, Ryan, really get away and talk to him."

"You really think it's a good idea, don't you?" I asked.

"Yes. If nothing else has worked, yes, I do."

"Steve said his grandfather has a cabin in Montana that might be available."

"Ryan, that's it. Look at all the times you've told me you wanted to go to Montana."

"Yeah, but I meant with you and the kids."

"You're always telling me things happen for a reason, right?"

"Yeah, so?"

"Maybe God wants you to go to Montana alone," she said. "I think this weekend happened for a reason, and part of it was to show us you're not healed. Something is at the root of your hurt, your pain, your fear."

Sarah had been paying attention to all of my sayings and beliefs. They were coming back to haunt me. "See, you have me believing you," Sarah teased. "Ryan, I believe with all my heart that God brought us together. And God didn't go to all this trouble for us not to make it." I looked at this angel before me, her love for me undaunted by the prior weekend's events. "You asked me to be patient and I will be. Just think about what I said."

I promised her I would think about it. If this would bring me peace and healing then maybe I should do it for her.

When I arrived home, the night air was filled with the fragrance of honeysuckle. I opened the back door to let Red out. While he scurried around the property, taking in all the scents, I stood looking out into the darkness. I breathed deeply the heavenly aroma. Red ran back and sat by my side. "How are you doing, boy?" I said. He wagged his tail, showing his pleasure to be with me. My thoughts wandered to Sarah's comments. I looked to the night sky and wondered what God wanted me to do. Were these events predestined by him, and if so why? I bowed my head in prayer. "Dear Lord, show me what to do, for I am lost. Nothing I've done has worked. Please, Lord, I hope you hear me for I need you now." I opened the door and followed Red into the house. That night, as I drifted off to sleep, Sarah's words played in my head. *Maybe God wants you to go to Montana alone.*

But I didn't want to go alone.

CHAPTER TWELVE

Steve arrived at two o'clock on Friday, as promised.
On the way to the doctor I shared my conversation with
Sarah.

"Oh, by the way, I checked with my grandfather
and the cabin is yours, if you like. He just needs a few
days' notice to get it ready," Steve said.

"I don't know," I said. "I'm not really into making
a long trip like that by myself. I don't even know what I'd
do there, and it's such a long trip."

"Hey, I don't know either, buddy. But you've
been a bit of a wreck lately and maybe Sarah knows what
she's talking about."

"But seriously, why would I find answers in Montana when I can't find them here?"

"I don't know, but I've heard the saying many times: God works in mysterious ways," he said, laughing.

"I just can't see me doing it," I replied."

The doctor examined my eyes and took some measurements for my upcoming Lasik surgery. "Ryan, I'm perplexed about your results on the full-vision field."

"Why?" I asked.

"Something isn't right. "See here," he said, pointing to the results of my peripheral vision test. "These circles should be all white."

I looked and saw a lot of dark area. "What's it mean?"

"It tells me your peripheral vision isn't what it should be. Do any of your relatives suffer from eye disease?"

I sat motionless, almost afraid to answer. Finally, I said, "Yes—some of them did have RP."

"Retinitis Pigmentosa," he said. "I can't say for certain, but let me take a closer look since your eyes are dilated.

"How can this be?" I gasped. My mind raced in terror. Several of my relatives had gone blind from RP, my cousin by the age of thirty-six.

"Usually we can tell from routine eye examinations, but in your case it isn't showing. I don't know why," he said, trying to be compassionate.

"Could it be anything else?"

"I seriously doubt it. But let me take a closer look." After several minutes the doctor finished the examination. My heart pounded as he rolled his chair over and turned on the lights. He positioned his chair in front of me and confirmed it: I had RP.

I was stunned. RP scared the hell out of me, and there was no cure. *What is happening to my life?* I screamed in my head. The doctor was still talking, but I didn't hear a word he said. Why, of all times, was I getting news like this now?

I put on a brave face and even tried to crack a joke, but inside I was breaking. I thanked him as I left. What was I thanking him for?

"Ryan, hey, what's going on?" Steve said as he followed me to his car. "You look like hell, what happened in there?"

I stood next to his car, shaking my head in disbelief. Finally, I banged my fists on the roof. "Why, God? Why me?" I shouted. "Why?"

"Ryan, what the hell is going on?" Steve asked again.

"Just take me home. I'll tell you when we get there," I said. "Just let me be till we get there, please. I need a few minutes."

"Sure, whatever you want," Steve replied, still dumbfounded by my behavior. As we drove to my place, I sat in silence, drowning in my reality. One week ago my life seemed filled with love and joy and hope, and now it was spiraling out of control. A tidal wave of hopelessness crashed into me.

Steve pulled in the driveway and stopped the car. His eyes were focused on me. "C'mon in," I said. "I need a drink, a strong one." I poured us each a glass of bourbon. I took a big gulp. "You, too," I said, pointing to his glass. He did the same.

Looking across the table at my best friend I shared my heartbreaking news. "I have a good chance of going blind, can you believe that?" I said, taking another drink. My hands shook.

"I don't understand. I mean, how?"

"Heredity, Steve. Heredity. It runs in my family and it turns out I have it."

"Are you sure?"

"Yes, I am," I answered, almost whispering.

"Can't they do anything?"

"No, buddy. No they can't. And you have to promise you'll tell no one, and I mean *no one,* especially Sarah," I said. "Promise me."

"I promise. But I think Sarah should know."

"Not yet. I'll tell her in time," I assured him. "Damn it, I don't need this now. What am I going to do?" I poured myself another drink and held the bottle toward Steve.

"No thanks, I have to drive," he said.

"I know you do," I replied. "I'm sorry. I just don't know what I'm going to do," I said.

"Is there anything *I* can do?" he asked. "Anything?"

I let out a sigh, and half-heartedly said, "Call your grandfather."

"Is that all? Are you serious?"

"Look, I know you want to help, but I need to be alone." I said.

"I understand," Steve replied. "I'll call him. And call me if there's anything else I can do."

"I will," I promised. "And remember, not a word of this to anyone."

After he left, I fell back into the kitchen chair. I picked up my glass and stared at the liquor inside. My world was falling apart. Anger coursed through my veins. I shattered my glass against the kitchen wall. Red, terrified, ran into the living room. "Damn you!" I yelled, pointing my finger to the ceiling. "What are you doing to me?" I banged my fists on the table, out of control. I kicked the kitchen chair over and upset the table, cursing everything in sight. I picked up Steve's glass and threw it against the cupboards. I slouched against the countertop, teeth clenched in anger. Red trembled in the doorway, his tail between his legs. I fell to the floor and burst into tears. "Why me, God? Why me?" The words struck me cold. I remembered crying out the very same thing when my stepmother beat me. The anguish, the pain, the hopelessness flooded back until I was a heartbroken child all over again.

I laid there sobbing, drowning in my own self-pity, when I felt Red's nose against my cheek. I crawled to my knees and wrapped my arms around his neck. "I'm sorry, boy. I'm so sorry for scaring you." His tail thumped against the floor at the sound of my words. "It's okay, boy, it's okay now," I said softly, patting his head.

I pulled myself to my feet. I could barely remember my fit of rage, but my kitchen bore testimony to my anger. I was numb. I couldn't feel a thing. I stumbled into the living room, fell on the couch, and finally passed out.

I had the strangest dream. An old man stood off in the distance by a woods. He kept yelling to me, telling me not to be afraid, and to take the journey. I yelled back, "What journey?" but the old man turned and walked away. And then I heard that voice in my dream, the same voice I first heard in church that Sunday. *Stay true to the path I've put you on. Trust in me.* I whirled around and saw a figure fading away. I turned back around and the old man was gone. Suddenly I woke up, dazed and confused. Then my eyes looked into the kitchen and reality hit me right between the eyes. It hadn't all been a dream. I still felt numb. It was as if I was watching someone else's life. but, as I picked up the table and chairs and cleaned up the broken glass, I knew too well it was my life I was watching.

That night I had the same dream again. The same old man telling me not to be afraid, take the journey. And the same voice. *Trust in me.* And when I turned to face the voice, again the figure faded quickly away. Who was it? What did this all mean? I was soon to find out.

CHAPTER THIRTEEN

The next week went by in slow motion. I was still reeling from the previous week's events. I couldn't concentrate at work or at home. Somehow, I thought, a rational solution would miraculously appear, but it didn't. I was still grappling with the reality of it all. My future seemed bleak. I wondered how Sarah would react to the knowledge of me slowly losing my sight. My hopes and dreams for the future all lost their substance. And at night, the same recurring dream, night after night. Was I having a nervous breakdown? Maybe the news of my impending blindness had finally pushed me over the edge.

I woke up in a cold sweat. I went to the bathroom to wash my face. When I looked in the mirror I barely recognized the man who looked back at me. There was no sparkle in his eyes, no smile on his face. The man I stared at looked as if life itself had been drained out of him. Was this really me?

The urge to take this trip wouldn't release its hold on me. Part of me fought it because I was in no mood to make the journey. My nights were restless and I started to look like hell. Even my co-workers worried that I was sick. I found myself talking to myself when I was alone. I thought for sure I was cracking up.

This night would push me to make a decision. Again, I had the dream with the old man yelling, "Take the journey," and the voice in my head, *Trust in me*. I ignored both of them. Then the dream took a bizarre twist. This time, all the people dear to me stood on the edge of a deep ravine. One by one they dropped off the edge. In the distance were four people I didn't recognize. I ran towards them, screaming for them to get away from the edge. Suddenly I could see their faces. Their hands reached out to me as the ground beneath them started to break away. Horror screamed through my mind, for it was Sarah, Brent, Elisha, and Lindsay. The dearest people in my life were slipping away from me. I screamed, "No-o-o-o-o! No-o-o-o-o!"

I woke up soaked in sweat, trembling. Just the thought of losing them terrified me. I laid there for the longest time when it finally hit me: The dreams, the voices, were they a warning? I was more afraid of losing them then taking this trip.

The next day I met with Allen, my supervisor. I apologized for the short notice, but I needed to take a leave of absence. I told him I needed a month and he said that was fine, and then added, "You look as if you could use it." I would leave Sunday morning.

I called Sarah and asked her to stop by Saturday evening so we could talk. Meanwhile, I set everything up with Steve and he gave me a map with directions to his grandfather's cabin. "Help Sarah take care of things, will you?" I asked.

"Hey, no problem, buddy. I wish you luck, and keep in touch."

I thanked him for everything and for being my friend.

Sarah arrived around seven on Saturday evening. "Ryan, you sounded so serious on the phone, I'm almost afraid to ask what this is all about," she said hesitantly.

"You deserve someone better than me. Maybe you'd be just better off without me," I said dejectedly.

"No, I wouldn't," she snapped back. "What kind of talk is that?"

I hung my head. "I don't know. Maybe I'll never feel secure in any relationship," I said. "And that's not fair to you."

"Why don't you allow me to be the judge of what's fair to me, okay?" she said softly. "What can I do to help? There must be something I can do."

"What more could you possibly do?" I asked. "You've been so patient and understanding already. What more could you do or want to do?"

"How about a little more patience and a little more understanding?" she said, smiling. I couldn't help but smile back.

"Sarah, I feel like I'm going crazy. I keep having these dreams, the urge in me to leave is always there. I'm going to Montana." She put her hands over her mouth as if shocked by my news. "You advised me to go," I said at her reaction.

"I know, I know," she said. "I, well, it's—it's just so sudden."

"Sarah, right now my life's a mess. *I'm* a mess. I can't think straight. I don't sleep at night except long enough to have those damn dreams over and over."

"Is there something you're not telling me?" she asked. "I mean, you seem different. You seem sad."

"Right now, I *am* pretty sad."

"Your feelings for me haven't changed, have they?" she asked.

I was surprised by her comment. "No, Sarah, no. I love you very, very much."

"I love you too, and my feelings haven't changed," she assured me. "I somehow feel responsible for all this"

"That's ridiculous. I'm the one with the problem, and I have to deal with it. Our weekend away certainly proved that," I said.

"How long are you going for?" she asked.

"I asked for a month off at work. I'm leaving to-morrow morning" I said.

She started to cry. "I miss you already," she said through her tears. I reached over and hugged her.

"I'll miss you, too," I said. "My plan was always for you to come with me."

"I will next trip," she replied, smiling. "What are you going to do with Red?"

"I'm taking him with me."

"You're what?" she asked, surprised.

"It's just easier for me to take him since I'm going to be gone so long," I said.

"I'd be happy to care for him."

"I know you would, but I figure he can be my eyes and ears at night. I mean, I have no clue where I'm going or what's waiting for me out there." Though I felt the need to go on this trip, my heart still wasn't in it. "I really don't want to be alone tonight. Would you mind staying?"

She squeezed me tightly, smiled, and said, "You couldn't have gotten me to leave."

Sarah helped me finish packing. I was glad she was there. She was my glimmer of light in the dark cloud of despair that suddenly hung over me.

That night I savored every moment of holding her in my arms. I didn't ever want to let go. Her love and warmth comforted me. Did I truly know what I was doing? Why was it so important that I go? What invisible force was driving me to go? I smiled as I thought about Sarah saying it was my guardian angel guiding me. I hoped she was right.

CHAPTER FOURTEEN

I awoke Sunday morning as the first ray of sun streamed through my window. I breathed deeply, trying to separate dreams from reality. Part of me truly dreaded leaving. Part of me fought the invisible urge to take this trip. No matter how hard I fought, there was no escaping the feeling of urgency to go. I was scared.

I went downstairs, put some coffee on, and let Red out. The morning sun greeted me in a shower of warmth. I breathed in the clean air, listening to the birds singing. I would miss my home. I stared into the woods, wondering about the mystery that awaited me. I even wondered if this might be the last time I would feel home again. I shook the thoughts of doom from my mind. *Face it like a man,* I told myself, but it didn't make it any easier to go.

I felt her hand touch my shoulder. I turned to see my beautiful Sarah. "Morning," she said, wrapping her arms around me. "How are you doing?"

"I'm doing okay," I said. I don't think she was buying my act, though.

"I heard you dreaming last night. Was it the same dream?"

"Yes and no."

"You woke me with your screaming. I was worried."

I looked into her eyes. "I dreamed I lost all of you last night, and I couldn't save you. It scared the hell out of me," I said. "What does all this mean? I . . . I don't get it."

She smiled. "I think your guardian angel is making sure you go on your trip." She kissed my cheek. "Everything will be all right. Have faith."

Her loving gentleness eased my anxiety. We walked inside. She poured our coffee and made breakfast. I showed her the route I would take to Montana and she quizzed me on my packing.

I walked Sarah out to her car. "You sure you don't want me to help put your things in the car?" she asked.

"No, but I appreciate the offer. This is hard enough," I said. "Having you here when I leave will only make it tougher. And you would cry," She already was. She knelt and hugged Red.

"You look out for Ryan," she said, patting his head. She wrapped her arms around my neck and laid her head on my shoulder. We stood for a long time just holding one another, soaking in the oneness that we felt. Slowly she lifted her head and looked up at me. I wiped her tears from her face. "Ryan, you are a very special man, and I love you very much. God has special plans for you, I can feel it. My thoughts and my prayers will be with you every day. God, I don't want you to go."

"Everything will be okay, you said so yourself." I forced a smile, and she smiled back. I gave her another kiss before she got in her car.

"You call me as soon as you get there, you promise," she insisted.

"Yes, I promise. I love you," I said. I waved as she drove away. She was crying again.

I slowly walked back to the house. My heart ached for what this was doing to Sarah. I loaded my gear and supplies. My mind searched for a rational answer for this trip but found none. It didn't matter. I was going whether I wanted to or not.

I locked up the house and called Red to the car. I motioned for him to get in and he barked his excitement. I started the car. "Boy," I said, patting his head. "You're in for the car trip of your life." So was I.

CHAPTER FIFTEEN

An air of unease hung over my departure. Never before in my life had I planned a trip of this magnitude, especially on such short notice. And the larger question still loomed before me: Why did I feel compelled to go? Was there some divine power at work guiding me to the answers I sought? My irrational fear of marrying Sarah had thrown me. How would this trip provide a solution? My love for her was so strong that I would try anything to rid myself of the anxiety and fear that paralyzed me. *And maybe, Lord,* I thought, *I'll discover somewhere in the wilderness why you have so forsaken me.*

As we pulled onto the turnpike to head west, it started to rain. The sound of the wipers slowly faded as I got lost in my thoughts again. The miles clicked past one after another as if I were in a fog. We stopped briefly along the road to stretch. Red was thoroughly enjoying himself, and gave me a look as if to say, *Why aren't you?*

The sky started to clear as we neared the end of the Pennsylvania Turnpike. We arrived at our campsite, an hour into Ohio, around six-thirty. I set up the tent and built a fire. I started cooking supper. The smell of steak and potatoes cooking in the great outdoors did help lift my spirits. After dinner, I poured myself some coffee and sat by the fire, just trying to relax. Red curled up beside me. I leaned back, closed my eyes, and tried to clear my mind of its jumbled thoughts. Dusk settled in, and the crackling fire sent embers dancing in the air. I wrote a few thoughts in my journal. If I was going to find answers I needed to be open-minded to everything along the way. I made a note that I wondered if this might be the start of me losing my mind. I shook my head as I put my pen down. The weight I had felt had returned.

I laid out a blanket for Red while I unrolled my sleeping bag. I checked the fire once more then crawled into my sleeping bag and patted Red. "Boy, I'm glad you're here with me," I told him. He wagged his tail in approval. From the door of the tent I could see the low dancing flames of the fire. A sense of loneliness set upon me—that same scary sense of being totally alone that had haunted me for so many years. I wondered what my future held. I didn't feel very optimistic.

Over the next two days my despair continued to grow. A sense of depression consumed me as we passed through one state after another. I barely remembered anything along the way.

By Wednesday we were over halfway to Montana. My thoughts turned to the letter I had sent Sarah. *She should get it today*, I thought. Will my words make sense to her? Will they help her understand me? I wondered how, over the past year, I could feel so alive and filled with love, and then a single event could stir up my feelings of insecurity and worthlessness. I couldn't even turn to God for help because I was sure he wasn't listening. What was the purpose of our being here, anyhow? I sank deeper into a pool of hopelessness. I struggled to fight it, but everything I had learned over the years from countless self-help books and motivational seminars had deserted me. My lifeline to reality was quickly unraveling.

On Friday morning we crossed the border into Montana. The despair wouldn't go away; The pool of self-pity was swallowing me up.

I had been driving since four-thirty a.m. and we still had a long drive ahead of us, so I pulled off the road to rest.

I reclined the driver's seat and closed my eyes. Red put his nose against my cheek. "Good boy," I said, patting his head. "Now lay down, we're going to take a little break before we head on." Red nuzzled me again, then laid down in the back seat.

I had the strangest dream. I had been hiking and had come to a cliff. Red pranced around me, lost his footing on the edge, and fell off. I dove to grab him, but missed. Then he floated back to the top of the cliff as if held by some invisible force. A voice came from behind me. "You are not staying true to the path, and you have allowed your faith in me to all but disappear. You have raised your fists in anger at me and have even sworn at me, but I shall not desert you in your time of need. I never have in all your years." Then an intense light flashed in my eyes, blinding me for a moment. I backed away from the cliff and jumped back in surprise. Standing before me was a tall old man. I was sure he hadn't been there before, but I also hadn't heard him approach. He had white hair and wore old clothes, brown pants with a faded yellow shirt and an old brown sport coat. The left sleeve was torn. "Who are you?" I asked, still shaken by his sudden appearance.

"Who I am is not important now. Know that when you have reached the edge of your cliff in life and are about to slip over, I will be sent to save you."

"Save me from what?" He looked down at me, silent, his brown eyes filled with sadness. "Save me from what?" I repeated. He only turned and walked away.

I chased after him, screaming, "Save me from what?"

He turned and answered in a deep voice. "From yourself and your disbelief."

Then he disappeared. I tried to understand his answer. Red stood where the old man had been, barking louder and louder until I could no longer take the noise. Someone was tapping my shoulder.

"Sir, sir, wake up. Are you okay?" I slowly focused my eyes to see a man in uniform standing outside my car. I jerked up in my seat, startled. He said, "It's okay, sir. I'm with the Montana Highway Patrol. Is everything okay here?"

Shaking my head to chase away the sleep, I answered, "Yes, officer, everything's okay. I must have fallen asleep. I pulled off to rest and must have dozed off."

"You were really out of it, it took me awhile to wake you. You haven't been drinking, have you?"

"No, no, but I did just have the strangest dream."

He opened my door. "Why don't you walk around and get your blood circulating. I saw you were from out of state so I stopped to see if you needed some assistance."

"Hey, I appreciate you doing that. it's my first visit to Montana."

I told him where I was going, and he confirmed that I still had a long drive ahead of me. He reminded me to stay alert because there was no daytime speed limit. He gave Red a pat on the head, wished me luck, and drove away.

I forgot my troubles during our brief conversation. They soon returned, weighing me down in despair. Whatever it was I came out here searching for, I apparently hadn't found it yet. In fact, I felt even more lonely than I did when I left. *What the hell am I doing here?* I wondered.

My thoughts returned to my dream. What did it all mean? Did it mean *anything?* I certainly felt as if I were hanging from an emotional cliff. And how could this old man save me? I finally pushed the dream from my thoughts.

The further I drove the more scenic the route became. As the lines on the road flicked by like dots, I could see snow peaked mountains off in the distance. I took a deep breath and exhaled as the speedometer reached eighty.

We took a lunch break for several hours. I took Red for a walk down by a small lake behind the restaurant. I sat down beneath the canopy of a large oak tree. A cool breeze brushed past my face. I looked to the sky. *God, will I find what I'm looking for? I hope I know it when I see it. You're probably not listening anyway.* I quickly changed my train of thought.

At about six-thirty I came upon a tavern housed in a large log cabin. I don't know why, but I decided to stop. I could definitely use a drink. I parked at the edge of the lot down by the trees so Red would be in the shade. The evening was turning cool, so I knew he'd be okay in the car, and I wouldn't be long anyhow.

After a couple beers and a shot chaser I laid my head down on the bar. The evening wore on and the place became more crowded. Before I knew it, several hours had passed. The alcohol helped numb the pain, but it did absolutely nothing for my depression. I headed for the door.

As I neared the car, Red started barking frantically. I thought he was excited to see me, but my dulled senses failed to pick up a crucial detail: This was a different bark. A sharp, intense pain to the side of my head and I fell to the ground. Things got fuzzy. Red's barking. Muffled voices. I tried to get up, but I couldn't. A boot in my chest and a kick to my head. Hands going through my pockets. Then everything went black.

PART TWO

PART TWO

CHAPTER SIXTEEN

I awoke with my head exploding in pain. My arms and legs were numb. It hurt to even breathe. My vision was blurred; I tried to focus on where I was. I groaned in agony. *Be still*, said a deep and gentle voice. A figure stood beside me. I strained harder to see and my eyes slowly adjusted. An old gentleman was next to my bed.

"Who are you?" I whispered. "Where am I?"

"Try to be still," he replied. "My name is Pete. I'm a doctor. Can you tell me your name?"

"Ryan Samuels," I moaned. "What happened?"

"You've been beaten pretty bad," he answered, "but you'll be all right."

I tried to sit up, and excruciating pain shot through me. "Don't," the old doc instructed. "Your ribs are badly bruised and you have a deep laceration on your head. You need rest." He turned to the door. "Charlie, Charlie," he yelled. "Come in here."

I felt like a Mac truck had run over me. Never had I experienced pain like I felt now. My vision had cleared considerably, and I heard footsteps walk to the doorway. He was a tall, big man. "Has our friend come around?" he asked the doctor. His voice seemed strangely familiar. He walked over to where I was. "How are you doing, friend?" he asked in a burly voice. I stared at him in disbelief. I couldn't get any words to come out of my mouth. I rubbed my eyes and opened them again. His clothes were different, but this was the old man in my dreams. No, it couldn't be. My mind raced for an explanation, an answer. *It must be the beating I took. I'm imagining things. I must be.* The old man noticed the shock on my face. "Doc here says you're going to be okay," he said. "Don't be frightened, you're among friends." Surprisingly, his words and his voice soothed me.

"My dog, is my dog okay?" I asked.

"Yes, he's fine," the old man answered. "He's right here lying on the floor next to your bed."

"Red, thank God you're okay." His tail wagged against the floor at the sound of his name.

"I've given you something for the pain," the doc said. "Now, it took twenty-three stitches to sew up your head, so you're going to have a good headache for a day or two . . . and there's a chance you've suffered a concussion, also. Charlie is going to keep a close eye on your through the night."

"Who did this?" I groaned.

"Don't know," Charlie answered. "They took off when your dog clawed his way out of your car. That's all I saw. The doc said you won't be able to travel for a while, at least a week or two." The pain medication was kicking in and I was fading fast.

"Charlie will take good care of you," I heard the doc say. "You're lucky he came by when he did. Now you get plenty of rest." Red walked over and sat by my bed, his eyes searching for assurance that I would be okay. I reached my hand over and patted his head. "That's some dog you have there," the doc continued. "He probably saved your life." They were the last words I heard before losing consciousness again.

The old man was sitting beside my bed when I awoke. He closed his book and walked over to me. He was a big man. My head felt like a train was running through it. "Oh, my head," I said, moaning.

"Welcome back to the real word," the old man said with a smile. "You had us a little worried."

"Why?" I groaned. "How long have I been asleep?"

"Nearly two days. The doc was here yesterday, but he didn't want to disturb you, so he told me to keep a close eye on you because of your concussion."

"You've been sitting here the whole time?" I asked.

"Pretty much." He got up and poured me some water. "Try to drink some," he said. I tried to sit up and the pain in my chest knocked me back down. "Here, try this," he said, putting another pillow under my head. "You're still in a lot of pain, aren't you? These pills the doc left should give you some relief. Also, I made some soup. Now take these pills while I go get it."

As I watched him leave the room, I still couldn't get over how similar he was to the old man in my dream. *Nonsense,* I thought. I looked around the room. It was simply furnished in a rustic decor. The wood floor and ceiling, and the log walls, told me that this was likely a log cabin. The room was neat and clean. Red lay on a rug by the bed.

I looked through the bedroom doorway into the living area. I could only see the far wall, and it was filled with books. I wondered, who was this kind gentleman who, without hesitation, was willing to care for a stranger?

Then it struck me. I had promised Sarah that I'd call and let her know I had arrived okay. If I had slept for the past two days, today had to be Monday. I told Sarah I would call her Friday night or Saturday at the latest.

The old man came in with a tray. I could smell the aroma of the soup.

"Charlie, I need to call my girlfriend. She has to be worried." I said frantically. He looked at me and smiled.

"We've already contacted her," he replied. "She knows you're okay."

"How? Who called her?" I asked.

His big hand rubbed his chin. "You don't remember, do you?"

"Remember what?"

"While you were really out of it, you kept mumbling about calling a *Sarah*. I kept you conscious long enough to get her telephone number."

"No, I don't remember," I said. "Is she okay?"

"She's fine and said for you not to worry. Oh, and that she loves you."

He leaned over and kissed my cheek. I looked at him strangely. "Oh, she asked me to give you that," the old man said with a smile. "She sounds like a special lady."

"She is. She really is."

"Oh," he said, remembering something more he needed to tell me. "She also said that she would contact your friend so he could tell his grandfather that you wouldn't be arriving for at least a week."

Great, I thought, as I sipped some soup. I come all the way out here in search of who knows what, and I wind up getting beaten by a couple of punks. *What is the purpose of all this?* I wondered.

And the more I saw and heard this old man, the more I sensed a connection to him. And, oddly, I felt like I belonged here. None of this made any sense.

There was a knock on the door. "Hi, c'mon in, the old man said. "Your patient is waiting for you." Doc Pete strolled into my room and Charlie stepped out.

"How are you doing today?" he asked cheerfully.

"I still feel pretty rough," I answered, "but my head doesn't hurt quite as much."

"Good, good," he said as he checked me over. "We'll take those stitches out in a few days. I see Charlie's taking good care of you."

"Yes, yes, he is," I replied. "I'm very grateful to both of you. Can I ask you a question, though?"

"Sure, what would you like to know?"

I motioned for him to close the door.

"Who is Charlie?" I asked, "and why is he being so kind to me?"

"Oh, Charlie is a dear and special friend," he replied. I could see the love he felt for this man by his expression and his comments. "Don't worry, son. You're in very special company."

"How so?" I asked.

"Oh," he said, smiling. "Old Charlie is one of God's angels on Earth." I stared, my eyes questioning him. "You'll find out in time, my friend." He told me he'd be back in a couple of days and to get plenty of rest until then. He opened the door to leave and then turned around. "Oh, you want to know where you are?" He looked at me for a moment, then he smiled. "Welcome to Charlie's Woods." Then he turned and closed the door.

"Charlie's Woods," I said aloud. *What's Charlie's Woods? What's so special about this place?* I wanted some answers. And I was about to get them.

CHAPTER SEVENTEEN

I did a lot of sleeping over the next couple of days. The old man took care of me cheerfully, preparing my meals, and helping me in and out of bed to visit the bathroom.

There was definitely something different about him. A genuine gentleness and kindness just flowed from him. Though I had stayed with him just these few days, I couldn't shake the feeling that I had known him a long time. The doc was right, and though I didn't understand or have an explanation for my feelings, I knew I was in very special company.

I was tired of lying in bed, so Charlie helped me to the living room. Well, it was more like a living room/dining area. I sat down at the table. Though I was still in much pain, it felt good to be out of bed.

Charlie went to the kitchen to make some tea. I looked around the room. In the center of one wall was a stone fireplace flanked by two rocking chairs. The walls were filled with books—lots and *lots* of books. A print of the crucifixion of Christ hung over the fireplace. As my eyes met the picture, a feeling of sadness swept over me.

Charlie returned, interrupting my thoughts. He set down our cups of tea and sat in the chair across from me. "Beautiful painting, isn't it?"

"Yes, it is," I said

"How's your tea?"

"It's very good," I answered. "What kind is it?"

"Oh, a special brew of my own. It's good for the soul."

Well, I need plenty of this, I thought. Red came over and sat next to me. "I think I owe you a big thank you," I said, rubbing his head.

"He's a beautiful dog," Charlie commented, "and I can tell he loves you very much."

"He's pretty special to me," I replied.

"Well, he and I have become good friends, but he wouldn't come out of your room except to go out. You must be very special, Ryan, to have an animal bond with you like that.

I nodded and then the words came out, and I don't know why. "I don't feel very special," I said, looking down at the table. I could feel the old man's eyes staring at me. I looked up. His eyes pierced the depths of my being.

"I sense you're troubled," he said kindly. "Would you like to talk about it?" I shook my head. Suddenly the reality of my life flooded back and the weight of my despair landed on my shoulders. I felt terribly alone, sitting in a strange house in the middle of nowhere.

He reached his large hands across the table and placed them gently over mine. Compassion filled his voice as he spoke. "Son, I am here to help. Trust in me." Those words, *trust in me,* shot through me like a bolt of lightning. I stared at the old man and started trembling. He squeezed my hands. He knew what I didn't know, understood what I didn't understand. Suddenly I was overwhelmed, the dreams, the voices, the feelings, they were all too much for me to comprehend. But the connection was made.

I sat there unable to speak. My cup danced to the edge of the table from my shaking and crashed to the floor. Inside I was screaming, but not a single word fell from my lips. Slowly, I pulled myself to my feet.

I apologized for the broken cup. "Charlie, I need to go lie down," I mumbled. "I don't feel very well." The old man gently helped me to my bed, and then closed the door behind him. I tried to catch my breath. I wanted to run, but physically couldn't. I was stuck here. But where was here? Was I in a spiritual haven or the twilight zone? This was too bizarre to make any rational sense.

As I slowly calmed down, my thinking became more rational. *Trust in me.* As I heard those words again in my mind, a calmness came over me. It made no sense, but I truly did trust this old man. A deep, bonding trust, like a boy trusting his father—never truly understanding the depth of that trust, but never questioning it either.

How could I feel such a bond with an old man that I just met several days ago? I wondered if the answers I sought were really here. I stared out the window for a long time and finally drifted off to sleep.

I slept till the following morning. As I eased myself into a sitting position I noticed my level of pain had decreased somewhat. The clock next to my bed said 7:35. Red heard my movements and jumped into bed next to me. "Easy, boy," I said. Even though the pain had lessened, my ribs were still very sore. Someone knocked on my door. "Come in," I said. The old man opened the door and greeted me with a smile.

"How are you this morning?" he asked warmly.

"Better," I answered. "still sore, but better."

"Good, good." Red jumped off the bed and walked over to him. "Hi, boy, would you like to go out?" Red barked and ran to the door. "I think he's taken quite a liking to me," the old man said. He let Red out and came back to my room. "Do you need help getting up?" he asked.

"No, I don't think so. I'm going to try it on my own," I answered. I groaned in pain as I hung my legs over the side of the bed. Charlie walked towards me. "I'm okay, I'm okay," I said. Pushing up with my arms I stood up by myself for the first time in nearly a week.

"Bravo, bravo!" Charlie bellowed, clapping his hands. I smiled at this curious old man. "Breakfast will be on the table in five minutes. Oh, what a glorious morning!" he shouted in his deep jovial voice as he disappeared into the kitchen.

I washed up and put on a bathrobe. Coffee and muffins were already on the table. Charlie pulled my chair out and he sat down across from me. He bowed his head. "Dear Heavenly Father, thank you for a new and glorious day. Thank you for the breath of life and all the wonderful possibilities that you lay before us on this new day. And Lord, we thank you for the food that is before us. I thank you for my new friend, Ryan, and we pray for his speedy recovery. And thank you, Lord, for those special gifts that you give us that are wrapped in disguise. We thank you for your love and compassion, your wisdom and kindness, your truth and your understanding. Lord, we thank you for all these blessings. Amen."

"Amen," I repeated, and picked up my coffee.

Charlie smiled at me. "Isn't life wonderful, Ryan?" he asked. I nodded half-heartedly. I wasn't thinking it was so great. He didn't push the point. "I need to go to town to pick up some supplies. It'll take me several hours. Will you be okay here alone?" he asked.

"I'll be fine."

"Good, good," he answered, taking our dishes to the kitchen. He poured me another cup of coffee. "It's a beautiful day to sit on the porch. Now make yourself at home."

I shuffled over to the screen door in time to see Charlie wave from his old truck as he backed around. Then down the road he went. The smell of the woods was invigorating, and the sun was already taking the morning chill away.

As I sipped my coffee, my curiosity got the best of me. I slowly examined my surroundings. Books were everywhere. In fact, except for a few pictures, they seemed to be his only possessions, and there must have been hundreds of them.

Books on religion, philosophy, biography; there were self-help books and books on meditation. There were shelves and shelves of books, and stacks of books on tables scattered around the room. I wondered if Charlie could possibly have read them all. "Red, he's either crazy or very wise," I joked. Since I was trapped in his home I was hoping for the wisdom scenario. Then I noticed a book sitting alone on a shelf in the comer. It was thick, wrapped in a soft red cloth. I walked over, almost as if I were drawn to it. My fingers slowly peeled the cloth away from it. In front of me lay the most exquisite Bible I had ever seen. The leather cover was beautifully ingrained and its pages were edged in gold. I wanted to hold it, but I dared not touch it. I couldn't explain why, but I sensed that this book was something very special.

The cabin was rustically and simply furnished. It was exceptionally clean. Except for the stacks of books, everything was neat and orderly. The wood floors were worn but spotless.

I walked out onto the porch and sat in one of the rockers. Red laid down beside me. As far as I could see was nothing but woods. Birdsong filled the air. A pair of chipmunks darted about, searching for food. The air was filled with the sweet smells of nature. I laid my head back and took a deep breath. It felt good to be outside.

But why was I here? And what made this place so special, as the doc put it? Oh, it was beautiful and serene, but my cloud of despair still hung over me. As I stared through the trees, I realized how hopelessly lost I was. Here I was, in my early forties, unhappy with my life, disappointed with where I was and what I had achieved, unfulfilled in my work, and afraid to commit my love to

Sarah. My life had lost its purpose and its direction. What would life be like when blindness finally overtook me? The sheer frailty of my body frightened me. All the negativity and hopelessness I was trying to escape were here all around me. Would I never find peace?

As I sat here among all this beauty my depressing reality had found me. Though I was thankful to be alive, part of me wished the thugs had killed me. I was tired, tired of pretending to be someone I wasn't, tired of dreams that wouldn't come true, tired of being afraid.

Out here there was no one to impress, no one to put up a brave front for, no one at all. I broke down and cried like a scared child stuck in a grown man's body.

While I drowned alone in a pool of self-pity, I seriously questioned the truth in any of it. Death didn't seem like such an irrational solution. I was tired, very tired, and just wanted the turmoil to end. *God, please help me,* I said.

A loud bang jolted me out of my despairing thoughts. A stiff breeze blew and I noticed a flowerpot broken on the porch. It had apparently fallen off the windowsill.

Then I realized how depressed my thoughts had made me. *God,* I thought, *why am I going there?* Here I was amidst nature's finest, surrounded by beauty and tranquility, and yet I couldn't feel it. I decided to take a little walk hoping the exercise would help chase my blues away.

As my steps fell into a slow progressive pace my mind began to wander. Well, more like someone else's thoughts trying to force their way into mine. I stopped and looked to the sky, my eyes greeted with a beautiful sea of blue. It felt as if God was smiling, and the feeling touched every part of my body. Then I felt ashamed for my self-pity and despair.

I heard a voice, but there was no sound. An image of the past dragged across my thoughts. I suddenly realized the fullness of the old man's kindness and compassion. Oh, I had thanked him, but was it truly from my heart? I had become so filled with my own hopeless situation that there wasn't much room for love and gratitude.

And I was being shown another side of this old man. I knew little of him, and there was certainly an air of mystique that surrounded him. Here was an old man who seemed totally grateful. Because of his few material possessions, most people would think him poor, but he seemed happy and at peace.

As I walked back to the cabin, I realized there was only one thing I could do. I hadn't come all this way to feel like this. It was time for the old man and me to have a talk.

CHAPTER EIGHTEEN

That afternoon the old man and I relaxed in the front-porch rockers. Charlie had been asking me questions since my arrival, but whenever he asked why I had come to Montana, I wasn't sure how to answer. Did I dare be totally honest and risk him thinking I was crazy? But there were too many coincidences to ignore. I looked over at him. He gently rocked, his eyes closed, his lips moving, but he didn't make a sound. He slowly opened his eyes and turned towards me. Noticing my stare, he chuckled. "Oh, I was just thanking the Lord for such a beautiful day. Oh, hallelujah!" he chimed.

"The fresh air certainly feels good," I said.

He leaned back in his rocker. "Close your eyes. Take slow, deep breaths. Now, thank God for the clean air filling your lungs. Give thanks for the very essence of life." After several minutes, I started to feel better, as if I was breathing in new life. "Good, good, Ryan," Charlie said. "I can already see that the power of thankfulness is working in you." I looked at him, puzzled. He smiled. "You're wondering what I'm talking about, aren't you?" he asked. I nodded. "Ryan," he said slowly, "the art of giving thanks is a powerful force, one that is too lacking in this day and age. You know, people have more today than they ever had before, and yet they aren't thankful. They've lost the meaning and significance of *being* thankful. And thus, no matter how much they have, it is never enough; they are never satisfied. *Oh, just a little more and I'll be happy,* they say." He shook his head. "What foolish thoughts fill their minds."

I listened to every word, as if drawn to them. He looked at me over his glasses. "don't you feel better now than you did earlier? At this moment, hasn't the power of giving thanks to God erased your depressing thoughts?"

I thought for a second and realized what he was saying was true. I asked, "How did you know what I was thinking and feeling earlier?"

"I just do. So many people spend their whole lives chasing an illusion of happiness. Oh, they think money, cars, big houses, all the material trappings of our world will bring them happiness, and yet they acquire all these things in abundance and at the end of their lives, happiness, joy, fulfillment has eluded their grasp. How ironic the secret to acquiring the joy they sought lived in their hearts in the love of God. They're like hamsters running in that metal wheel, forever running, but never really getting anywhere. They get caught in a cycle of greed and want that they never escape from. How sad."

I knew only too well what he was talking about. Despite my good nature and struggles to improve myself, I, too, had spent much time on that metal wheel. I had lost my appreciation for life. I had moments, now and then, of appreciation and gratitude for my blessings, but it never lasted. I had been chasing the illusion.

"Charlie," I said, "why are we like that? Why are we so ungrateful?"

"Because we lose our connection to our true self, our spirit, and to God. We get caught up in all the trappings of modern society and soon our entire self-worth, the way we measure life's value, is tied to our material wealth. When we have an abundance we become egotistical, selfish, and arrogant. When we have too little, we become depressed, mean, envious and cynical. And, like crabs at the bottom of a pot, we try to drag everyone else

159

down with us. And yet, when we think we have too little, we still have more than we ever really need. In this kind of life there is little or no room for love. All we're concerned with is what we haven't got and why." The old man shook his head. "And what's even sadder is we raise children with this attitude so they become cold and selfish, too. Growing up, they're lucky to ever get a glimpse of the true magnificence and power of love, *God's* love.

I could see the sadness in his eyes. "You know, Ryan, our children deserve so much better than that." I nodded in agreement.

Charlie got up and walked into the cabin. "I'll be back," he said. I sat there still feeling the impact of his words. Something was very different when Charlie spoke. I couldn't put my finger on it, but I was mesmerized every time he spoke. There was a genuine love and compassion that flowed from him that could not be resisted.

Maybe I didn't notice it before because of my physical anguish, but I was healing and my mental acuity was back. My sense of my surroundings was no longer a blur. Something was truly unique and special about Charlie. Maybe his talk made me realize how much I was already in his debt. After all, he had openly welcomed me into his home and had taken on the responsibility of nursing me back to health. I felt ashamed for, at first, I was suspect of his caring and kindness. Was this the attitude that recent decades had brought us to?

The slamming of the screen door jolted me out of my thoughts. Charlie smiled at me. He held two books. One was a tattered old Bible and the other was a worn-out paperback.

He turned towards me, looking over his glasses. "I know you have many questions. I'll answer them in time. But for now, I want you to take each day one at a time. And I ask you to remember that there are no coincidences in life. Everything and everyone who touches our lives has a meaning and a purpose. One of the secrets of life is opening your heart and mind to this reality."

"I've paid close attention to you since you arrived. I can sense the turmoil and despair that rages in you. I know your life is in crisis and that your very belief and faith in God is in question."

My mouth dropped open and I just stared at him. "How?" I finally muttered. "How do you know? How can you know what's inside of me? How?" I was starting to feel uneasy. Could he really know how lost and terrified I was?

Then, softly and gently, he responded. "Son, right now it's not important that you know how I know. Just remember that our lives didn't cross by coincidence, but by divine intervention." He smiled and put his hands on mine. I've been helping lost souls for half of my life, and you're in need of help, aren't you?"

"Maybe I am," I answered, "but I really don't feel like discussing it now." I just wasn't in the mood to spill my guts. I wasn't ready to acknowledge how much of a failure my life was. I lowered my head into my hands.

"That's okay," he said, patting my shoulder. "When you're ready, I'll be here." His kindness and understanding touched me. I sensed that, though a complete stranger, he truly did care about me. I felt bad for being so defensive. "I read these two books every day. I'd like to share a little of them with you."

"It's okay with me." He opened the maroon paperback first.

"This is my book of daily devotions," he said. As he read I tried to concentrate on his words, but thoughts of my own sad situation interfered. At the end of the page he closed his book and said, "Let us pray." I listened as he gave thanks to the Lord for all his blessings. And as he continued, my heart was pulled in by his words . . . His prayer was that of a common man communicating with God. He even thanked him for his problems! He prayed for the people he knew who needed God's divine help, and then he prayed for me. My emotions stirred as the words of his prayer poured forth. It was as if the old man had crawled inside my soul, for the essence of his words were my cry for help.

I wiped the tears from my face as we said *amen*. Then he then read a few passages from the Bible. Comfort enveloped me. When he finished, he handed his Bible to me. "Ryan," he said gently, "when you feel like it, read the first couple chapters from the Book of John."

"I will," I replied, "but I don't know what good it will do." He just smiled and walked into the cabin. I put the Bible on the wooden table beside me.

I leaned my head back in the chair and felt the warmth of the afternoon sun. A gentle breeze brushed my face. It was good to relax and I soon dozed off. Again I dreamed of standing by the cliff with Red. The ground crumbled and we began to fall. This time there was no old man to save us, just a voice saying, *Have faith and believe in me, for I am always with you. Reach out to me.* fading as we fell farther into the abyss.

The sensation of falling jerked me awake. I groaned in pain from the sudden movement. Charlie came to the door. "Are you okay, son?" he asked.

"Yes, just another dream. Why am I having these dreams all of a sudden?" I shouted. He just smiled and went back to whatever he was doing.

The old rocker creaked as I climbed out of it. I decided to take a little walk and shake loose the mental cobwebs. Red ran a short distance ahead. After a hundred yards or so, I sat on a stump next to a huge oak. I marveled at the size of the tree; its trunk was approximately six feet around and it had to be close to two hundred feet tall. How many hundreds of years had this old giant had been watching over the forest?

As I sat there in solitude, I lost myself in my thoughts. What was happening to me and where was I? Was it, as Charlie said, that I was here with him through divine intervention? There was a strange and mystical presence to this place, a sense, a feeling I couldn't explain. And because I didn't understand what was happening, a sense of fear ran through me, too. But, strangely, underlying my fear was a feeling of comfort, of being safe. I know it doesn't make sense, but it is how I felt.

Red barked as he chased a squirrel through the underbrush. At least *he* was enjoying himself. I called out his name as I began to start back. Then, as if out of thin air, was the old man. He startled me so that I nearly lost my balance. "I'm sorry, Ryan," he calmly said, "I didn't mean to startle you."

"How do you do that? Just appear like you do?"

No explanation, just that big warm smile. "Dinner is about ready, so I decided to come after you," he said.

"Thank you," I replied. "Red and I were just starting back." We walked the rest of the way in silence. I was still bewildered by his sudden appearance.

A lady came out the back door when we reached the cabin. "Betsy, Betsy!" Charlie bellowed. "How are you on this beautiful day?"

"I'm just terrific," she replied. Charlie introduced us and we exchanged greetings. "So you're the gentleman Charlie's taking care of," she said. "How are you doing?"

"I'm still a little sore, but I'm feeling better every day."

"Good, good. You're in wonderful hands," she said, smiling at Charlie. "Oh, I left you some fresh-baked bread to go with your dinner."

"You're an angel, Betsy." Charlie turned to me. "She bakes the best bread you've ever tasted. You're in for a treat!"

Betsy was a jolly, energetic lady who appeared to be in her fifties, her black hair streaked with gray. She chatted with us for a while and then said she had to be going. We said our goodbyes and watched her drive off.

Charlie told me that Betsy lived about a half mile down the road and stopped by once a week to chat and bring baked goods. "She's a wonderful cook," Charlie said, "and a wonderful lady. Her husband died a few years ago of cancer. Her visits always brighten my day."

As I sat down to dinner, Charlie brought in Betsy's bread. It was still warm and its heavenly aroma filled the room. He carefully sliced several pieces and delighted in the anticipation of his first taste. I watched as he closed his eyes savoring the bite. I couldn't help but laugh. He opened his eyes and smiled at me. "Go ahead," he gestured, "see what you think." The bread was as delicious as Charlie had said.

We laughed as we ate our meal. I hadn't laughed in weeks. I had almost forgotten how good it felt. Here, in these humble surroundings, this kind and gentle man made me feel both wanted and loved.

CHAPTER NINETEEN

I was awakened the following morning by Charlie's whistling and singing. As I got out of bed I noticed that the pain in my ribs had diminished. Moving was getting easier and less painful. Red greeted me as I opened the bedroom door and Charlie was right behind him. "Good morning, friend!" His booming voice filled the cabin. "And how are we on this beautiful day? Thankful, oh yes, thankful!"

"So am I," I replied halfheartedly as I closed the bathroom door. *Who is this old man?* I was still struggling between acceptance and resistance. *Why is he so happy?* He lived alone and, except for a bunch of books and his old truck, what did he have? And then it occurred to me: He had peace. Was it all because of his belief in God? I believed in God and my life was a total mess. What was I doing wrong? Could I learn the answers I desperately sought from this kind old gentleman? Somewhere deep inside I knew I need not travel any farther.

I looked in the mirror and barely recognized myself. I had been gone from home for over two weeks and hadn't shaved since I left. The stitches in the side of my head looked awful. I was glad they'd soon be out. I felt better, but I still looked pretty ragged.

As I walked to the table, Charlie greeted me with a smile. "Ah, yes, splendid. Yes, indeed, splendid!" he bellowed.

"What is?" I asked as I sat down.

"You. I can see you're getting around much better. How are your ribs?"

"They're still sore," I answered, "but the pain isn't nearly as bad."

"Good, good," he replied. "Oh, by the way, Doc will be by this morning to take out those stitches."

"I'm glad," I answered. "They look awful."

Doc arrived after breakfast. "How's my patient doing?" he asked.

"Still a little sore, but better."

Charlie poured a cup of coffee for his old friend and we chatted for a while. I liked Doc. He was warm and friendly and funny. "Do you always make house calls?" I asked.

"Oh, I do quite a bit out here," he answered. "People like to be treated in the comfort of their homes. I don't like being cramped in an old office anyhow."

He chatted with Charlie as he removed my stitches. Before I knew it, he was finished. I thanked him and asked how much I owed. "Not a dime. Charlie takes care of my fee so don't you worry about it." He packed his medical bag, wished us well, and said goodbye.

I watched him drive off. "He's such a nice man, and a terrific doctor. I know a few doctors who could learn a lot from old Pete," I said.

I pleaded with Charlie to allow me to pay something for the doc's care, but he would have none of that. "Doc and I have an arrangement," he said.

"But how do I thank you for all you've done for me?" I asked.

He looked out over his glasses and smiled. "I'll tell you how in time."

We returned to the table. Charlie's Bible and daily devotional were at his place and a somewhat newer Bible and devotional were at mine. We took turns reading and again Charlie prayed. His prayers were filled with gratitude. I always felt better after these readings, but how could I make the feelings last? I asked him. "I will teach you," he answered. Then he invited me to stay with him for the duration of my visit. I said I would and he smiled. I had come to like this old fellow and I felt I owed him something.

Again, he informed me he had errands to run and would be gone for several hours. I couldn't help but chuckle watching him drive off whistling and singing. If he weren't such a Godly man, I would swear he was on drugs.

I walked back in the cabin and looked through his books again. I was always amazed at the wealth of knowledge in his collection. Religion, philosophy, inspirational books from all the greats filled the room.

I knew I could learn from him, but what? And I still knew nothing about him except that he was special. I decided to try the half-mile walk to Betsy's. Maybe she could shed some light on him.

I wrote a note to Charlie in case he got home before I did and put it on the table. I told Red we were taking a walk and he exuberantly ran for the back door. As we walked, I was in awe of the peace and tranquility that surrounded us. I wondered what insights Betsy would share about Charlie. I only hoped she would be home.

We passed no other houses or people on the way. At last I could make out a house in the distance. "That has to be it," I told Red. Then I recognized her car in the driveway. Her house was a cottage-style with plants and flowers all around. A wind chime hung on the front porch, playing in the breeze.

I knocked on the door but no one answered. I walked around back. No one seemed to be around. Red barked and ran down in the woods. Then I heard her bubbly voice. "Back here!" she yelled, waving her arms. I waved back and walked toward her. "Good day to you," she said, smiling. "I'm so happy to see you. Where's Charlie?"

"Oh, he had some errands to run so we thought we'd come for a visit."

"Wonderful. It will give us a chance to talk." She placed the last of the mushrooms she had picked in a pail. "You're just in time for lunch." On the walk back to the house she shared memories of her beloved late husband, Frank. "We so loved this place," she said. "A little piece of heaven on earth." Her face lit up whenever she spoke of her husband.

"You must have loved him very much," I said.

"Oh, I still do. He's part of me and always will be," she said, patting her heart. "Come in, come in. You, too, Red." She led us to the kitchen and motioned for me to sit down. Her home was beautifully decorated, yet quaint. The kitchen was clean and neat as a pin. I instantly felt welcomed here.

"Are you married?" she asked as she cleaned the mushrooms.

"No, I'm divorced.

"Any children?"

"Yes, I have a wonderful son," I answered. "He stays with his Mom during the summer. He's ten years old and his name is Brent." I reached for my wallet to show her a picture, but I didn't have it with me. "What's that heavenly smell?" I asked.

"That's our lunch," she replied. "Fresh-made vegetable soup and bread." She sliced some of the mushrooms and added them to the pot. "It'll be ready shortly. I hope you're hungry." I was. My appetite had returned since the beating.

Betsy set the table and dished out our soup. She said grace and we proceeded to enjoy a delicious meal. I complimented her cooking expertise which she accepted very modestly.

"Is there a special someone in your life, Ryan?" she asked. I thought of Sarah and wondered how she was doing. I wasn't sure how to answer. Betsy noticed my silence. "I'm sorry, I don't mean to intrude," she said. "You just seem like such a nice young man I just assumed there was someone."

"That's okay," I replied. "I do have a very special lady in my life, I just wonder if she'll still be there when I get home." Betsy looked at me, questioning my comment, but didn't pry.

We chatted some more about her late husband and her children, and I shared where I lived and some details about my divorce. After lunch she invited me outside for some tea. There were pots of flowers placed around the deck. On one end a lattice was filled with flowering vines. Several hummingbirds darted about, filling themselves with the sweet nectar of the splendid red blooms. "It's so beautiful out here," I said.

"Yes, it is. "I thank God every day for the blessing of these woods."

"Charlie's Woods, right?" I asked with a chuckle.

"Why, yes," she answered, somewhat surprised. "You know about Charlie's Woods?"

"No, I don't. Just that Doc also refers to this place as Charlie's Woods. Doc told me this is a very special place."

"Oh, it is, it really is. I'll stay here until I die," she said happily.

"Don't you ever get lonely living out here?"

"Oh, my no. I love the peace and solitude. I feel so close to God out here. I've lived here now close to forty years. I have friends in town I visit, and they visit me from time to time, and Charlie, well, I couldn't have a nicer or friendlier neighbor. I'm truly content here." She gazed around her yard for a moment before continuing. "Charlie told me about you being attacked. What a shame. "hardly anything like that ever happens around here, so when it does it's shocking." I explained what had happened the best I could, and what my plans were. "Oh, I bet your plans are all ruined," she said sympathetically.

"Not really," I replied. "I had no concrete plans. I just had this compelling need to come out here in search of something, I'm not sure what. And now I'm in Charlie's Woods. Why does everyone call this Charlie's Woods, anyhow? I can't imagine he owns all this."

"Oh, but he does, as far as your eyes can see." My mouth dropped open in shock. Betsy laughed at my expression.

"I don't understand," I gasped. "He lives so modestly and drives that old truck. I thought all his worldly possessions were his books. How much land does he own?"

Betsy looked at me and smiled. "Nearly five thousand acres. See, money no longer matters to Charlie. In fact, upon his death, this land goes to the state of Montana on the condition that it's preserved in its natural pristine state as God created it. He has enough money to take care of his needs the rest of his life. The rest he gives away."

I sat there totally dumbfounded. "Betsy, I don't understand any of this. Please, please tell me about Charlie. I really need to know."

She poured more tea and handed me a plate of cookies. "Charlie grew up in New York City. His parents were poor immigrants from Germany. They worked hard and sent Charlie to the best schools. In fact, he graduated from Harvard, top of his class. He went to work on Wall Street and made a fortune. He fell in love, got married, and two years later their daughter was born."

"Where are they now?" I asked.

"Be patient," Betsy said, pointing her finger at me. Then she continued. "They had all the material trappings of life: money, cars, several homes, they had it all. Charlie adored his wife and daughter. They seemed like the perfect family. "Shortly after Beth—that's Charlie's daughter—turned twelve, she and her mother were coming home from a play. They were only a few miles from home when a drunk driver crashed head-on into their car.

Charlie's wife was killed instantly. Beth was critically injured, and in a coma. Charlie left his job to be with his daughter. He was by her side day and night for six agonizing months."

"What happened?" I asked, shocked by the story.

"Beth died. Charlie was devastated. He went into a downward spiral. He no longer paid attention to his business or personal affairs. He drank too much and became a recluse. To look at him, you would have thought him a bum, not a rich and powerful man. He had lost all appreciation for life. One night, late in the evening, he found himself wandering around the Brooklyn Bridge. He decided he had suffered enough. He wanted to be with his wife and his little girl. He was going to end his life. See, Ryan, he had lost something even more precious: his faith in God."

"Because of the accident," I said softly.

"Yes. He had prayed every day of those six months while Beth lay in a coma. And still she died. He became so angry with God, and his heart filled with hate until that hate sucked every last bit of life from him."

"What stopped him from jumping?"

"Well, as Charlie tells it, he was ready to jump when the squealing of tires distracted him. The car flipped several times, finally stopping on its roof less than fifty yards away. He heard a little girl cry out for help and ran to the car. She was bleeding and crying and trapped. He went to the other side of the car to check the driver; his face was turned toward him, but he was motionless— killed instantly. Charlie was filled with rage. It was the very same man who had killed his wife and daughter. He even thought for a second of leaving. *Why should I save your little girl?* he screamed. But the little girl's cries brought Charlie out of his rage. He couldn't leave her. He reached through the broken window and held her hand. He found himself suddenly praying for God to save this little girl. Suddenly, a bright light appeared over the car. A figure stood in the center of it, calling out to Charlie, *I am with her as I am with you. Be not afraid. She will be okay.* Charlie had been drinking and, at first, he doubted his eyes and ears. But then the light hovered over him. A feeling of warmth and love enveloped him. Never had he experienced such a pure and giving love. *Go home, for I have work for you to do. I will look after the girl.* Charlie got up and headed home. He turned back to see an ambulance pull up to the crash. The light that hovered over the car faded away.

"That night, Charlie tossed and turned, not able to get the vision out of his mind. The next morning, as he watched the news, he learned that the little girl was only slightly injured and the driver was dead at the scene. The report confirmed the driver's identity. The next night, the vision returned. He doesn't know if it was a dream or real, but he does know these visions saved his life. As the bright light appeared, he said there were three figures in the light. Two of them stepped forward out of the light. It was his wife and daughter. He sat up in bed reaching for them and calling their names. They told him they were fine and that they loved him. They told him not to worry and that they would see him again, but not now. *Listen to him,* they said as they stepped back into the light, into the third figure's outstretched arms. Then the light slowly faded away. When he awoke he was crying, but a feeling of peace and love filled his heart for the first time since their death."

I could hardly believe what I heard. "But how did he wind up here? What can he do out here in the middle of nowhere?"

Betsy looked at me and smiled. "The Lord's work," she said.

"How?"

"In another vision he was told to *live in harmony with nature and to love and teach those I send you. To love those souls who were lost and floundering on the edge of life.*"

A strange sensation coursed through me. "Why Montana? Why here?"

"Well," she continued, "several weeks went by and Charlie was trying to make sense of it all. He had regained his thirst for life and was driven by the visions he had witnessed, but he was also puzzled by them. Who would he be helping? And how? And live in harmony with nature? That really confused him since he lived in New York City all his life. Then one day, while reading a newspaper, he noticed a large ad in the real estate section: *FOR SALE 5000 acres of beautiful and pristine wilderness. A piece of Heaven on Earth.* Charlie took it to be a message from God. He contacted the owners, got his business affairs in order, flew out to Montana, and bought it on the spot."

I shook my head in disbelief. I had a new understanding and affection for this kind old gentleman. And then it hit me like a brick. I just stared at Betsy as I started trembling. She smiled and softly said, "You were chosen to come here, Ryan. You know that now, don't you?"

I could barely force my words out. "But why? Why me?" I said, nearly choking on the words.

My heart pounded and my mind raced. Now I understood the pull to come to Montana, but what was going to happen to me? Betsy noticed my anxiety. "Don't be nervous or afraid. I've seen this before."

"Seen what?"

"The other people who have come through Charlie's Woods. Some set of circumstances always leads Charlie to them."

"What happens to them?"

"All I can tell you is that their lives are forever changed. Be thankful, for you have been blessed by coming here."

I got out of my chair. "I've gotta talk to Charlie," I said. I felt like I was going to throw up. I thanked her for her hospitality, but I needed to go. I walked out her lane quickly. I would have run if I could. She called after me: "Ryan, remember, God loves you!"

My walk back went quickly. I was too numb to sense any pain. This was all too weird, and I was truly shaken by her story. What did she mean, *I was chosen?* Chosen for what? I wasn't anybody special. I felt as if I was being guided by forces I had no control over. Any peace that I had felt was gone. I was frightened and part of me wanted to run away.

My ribs started to ache as I neared Charlie's cabin. I got to the porch and fell back into one of the rockers. I slowed my breathing and started to calm myself down. I couldn't leave here. I knew that. Now I knew I belonged, and here was where I would find my answers, whatever they would be. Tonight the old man and I would talk.

CHAPTER TWENTY

Charlie pulled in the driveway about an hour later. I was still lost in a sea of thoughts. "Hello, my friend," he said in his usual cheery voice. "Are you enjoying this beautiful afternoon?"

"I guess so," I replied half-heartedly. I just wanted to sit him down and share with him everything Betsy had told me earlier. I had so many questions that needed answers.

The old man noticed my mood. "Are you okay, Ryan?" he asked with concern. "You seem troubled."

"I'm not sure of anything, Charlie," I replied.

"Did something happen while I was gone?"

I nodded. "Yes. Red and I paid Betsy a visit. I thought the walk would do me good."

"Oh," he said. "I'm sure she was delighted to see you. She doesn't entertain folks very often. And how was your visit?"

"It was interesting. We enjoyed a wonderful lunch together and had quite a chat."

"I see," he replied, looking over his glasses at me as if in thought.

The anxiety exploded inside of me as I relived her words in my thoughts. "Charlie, I don't understand what's going on here, the things Betsy told me." I was starting to tremble.

"I know, Ryan," he said. "I know."

"But," I started.

"Shhh. Please, son, be patient a little while longer. We'll talk after dinner, I promise," he said, looking into my eyes with compassion and understanding. He got up and headed for the door, shaking his head. I heard him mumble as he went inside, "That Betsy, she does go on."

He reappeared a good while later, informing me that dinner was started. I got up and went in the house and set the table. As I arranged the plates and silverware, I could feel Charlie's eyes upon me. The power of his presence could be overwhelming. My anxiety had subsided some, but I was still filled with so many questions about him and this place called Charlie's Woods. I didn't know how I would ever sit down to eat, but I knew I had to force myself. The old man's meals were never fancy, but they were always delicious. The smell of baking chicken stirred my appetite. When dinner was ready, he said grace and we began our meal in silence. Every now and then he'd look up and smile. The silence was driving me crazy. "Charlie," I finally said, breaking the silence. "We really need to talk."

"I know," he replied, looking out over those glasses of his. "After dinner, we have much work to do. Now try to enjoy your dinner."

I kept my eyes on Charlie through the rest of our meal. He seemed deep in thought, so I kept my mouth shut. We cleaned up from dinner and, since the evening air was turning cool, he asked me to start a fire. As I placed the kindling and wood in the fireplace, I kept wondering about what this special man would discuss with me.

Once I had the fire going, I went out and brought in a few more pieces of wood and stacked them in his wood box. Charlie held two glasses. "Would you please join me in having a refreshing drink?" he asked.

"What is it?"

"It's a very special tea that I make only for special occasions."

I agreed to join him. As he filled our glasses with the golden liquid a sweet fragrance filled my senses. He held his glass close to his nose and inhaled. I did likewise. It was heavenly and had an immediate soothing and calming effect.

He raised his glass to mine. "To friendship and love." While I am no connoisseur of fine drink, the taste filled my tastebuds with delight.

"Charlie, this is truly delicious and refreshing," I exclaimed. "What is it?"

"It's a very special blend of teas and herbs that a wise old friend introduced me too. The ingredients are very rare so I only make it on special occasions."

We both sat by the fire. The old man savored the simple pleasure of his tea, so I tried doing the same. But I needed some answers. The wait was excruciating.

After what seemed an eternity, he set his glass down. He turned his chair more towards me. "Ryan," he said, "I know you have many questions, even more so after today. If your heart is open and you truly trust in me, I will help you find your answers. There are so many people who, like you, are good and decent, but they have lost their way. In an effort to fill the emptiness in their souls, to relieve the pain in their lives, they turn down many paths searching for something. I'm sure you've traveled on some of those same paths, and all eventually lead to destruction. Drugs, alcohol, hatred, false pride, jealousy, and fear. Oh, yes, fear. Some become mean and abusive trying to make themselves feel better at others' expense. They lash out, criticize, gossip, lie, anything in an attempt to build their egos and their self-exaggerated importance. They all get so caught up in their destructive circumstances that they lose their ability to feel love, and compassion, and joy." He shook his head. "They try to keep building their lives on a foundation of sand instead of one of stone. They create a life of certain failure and eventually spend all the blessed energy of life on hate and blame and envy. Their lives become filled with excuses and they lose the consciousness of accepting responsibility for their choice in life. We all have choices, Ryan, every one of us. It's one of the true gifts from God, and the most dangerous: the total freedom of choice. And yet they still blame God for the emptiness of their lives."

I could identify only too well with his words. They hit pretty close to home. I was one of those lost souls.

He got up and stood by the fireplace. "All of them, including you, have so much to be thankful for, but their hearts have been blinded by their lack of faith and their lack of self-esteem." Now the old man was starting to lose me, and I certainly wasn't feeling any better. In fact, I was feeling ashamed. This wasn't how I expected him to make me feel.

He walked over and sat back down. "When we pray to God, we should always offer prayers of thanks, for in him is all we ever need. Too often, when we pray we're always asking for something, and when our prayers aren't answered in the way we expect, then God isn't real, God doesn't care. They'll even say he's an unloving God."

I could see the sadness in his eyes. He was quiet for a moment. I dared not say a word. I held so much re-spect awe for this wonderful old man, but I knew in my heart that I believed that God hadn't answered many of my prayers. How could I tell him that? I stared into the fire when he resumed speaking.

"Ryan, I am here to help you to a rebirth, a new life, if you will allow me. I can feel the unbelief in your heart and the despair in your soul. Let us take a minute to pray. Will you lead us in prayer?" he asked calmly.

I bowed my head, but I was unsure of what to say in the presence of such a wise and godly man. I was suddenly and unexplainably filled with a volatile mix of emotions. If I just uttered the words he would see through me, and I didn't share his unshakable faith. The silence became unbearable and the words wouldn't come. finally, I looked up and whispered, "I can't. I don't know why, I just can't." Charlie reached over to touch my hands and I pulled away. I didn't understand why I did. I did know the shame and inadequacy I felt could no longer be contained. I felt like a volcano ready to erupt. All my emotions were racing out of control. I was filled with anger and didn't know why. I couldn't even look at him.

"Just talk to God," he said. "He will listen. Unburden your heart to him."

I jumped out of my chair. "Maybe he listens to *you*," I shouted, "but He doesn't give a damn about me.

And you know *what?* I don't care about him either!" I screamed. "Who are you, anyway, and why do you even care?" I couldn't control myself. I felt as if I were possessed. Everything I'd been holding in came flooding out. "My life is a living hell," I yelled. "Is that how God has answered my prayers?" I spewed forth all the misfortunes of my life: the death of my mother as a boy, the abusive years with my stepmother, an unloving father, failed relationships, and insecurities. I was a madman.

"And do you know what the final blessing is that he's giving me?" I shouted, raising my arms and looking to the heavens. "He's letting me go blind." I looked at him coldly. "Now tell me how to thank him for all these blessings. You find the words. Go ahead, tell me what to say!"

He didn't blink an eye. He quietly listened to my ingratitude, my rudeness, my anger, and my pain. "Damn him, damn him, Charlie, why, why?" as tears flooded forth and I collapsed in his arms. He held me as I broke down, sobbing uncontrollably. "Why, Charlie, why has he deserted me?" All the pain and anguish of my years flooded out of me in a stream of tears.

As the old giant held me, he quietly whispered, "God's always been with you, son, trust me. Just let it all out."

"Charlie, I'm so sorry. I'm so ashamed," I whispered.

"It's okay, truly. This was necessary," he said. "This is a good thing, trust me. I slowly calmed down, but I was exhausted. The old man gently hugged me and said, "God loves you and so do I." I could feel his love emanate from him and wash over me. He finally let me go and I collapsed in the chair. I started to apologize again, but Charlie motioned for me to be silent. As I caught my breath, I felt a true sense of relief, like a huge weight had been lifted off my shoulders.

He gently placed his hands on mine. "Ryan, sometimes we need to get to the lowest point in our life, where we feel hopeless, afraid, and alone before God will truly allow us to witness his glory. Forty-two years ago I was where you are now. I know how you feel. I felt exactly the same anger and hopelessness. God chose to turn me around, and I didn't understand at the time either, but I certainly do now. I'm here to help you, son. Will you allow me?"

"Yes," I said.

CHAPTER TWENTY-ONE

Once I had calmed down I realized I had no energy left to hide or pretend. The only thing I could do was bare my soul to this man of God. I knew whatever was going to save me was right here with him. Quietly and calmly I unburdened my heart and relived the pain of my past—the anguish and confusion of losing my mother, the horrific abusive years with my stepmother, the longing to feel the love of a father who didn't know how to show it, the deep-rooted insecurities that led me to destructive and failed relationships.

I paused while the anguish of my past flooded over me once more. Charlie's expression echoed my pain. "Go on," he said, his gentle voice reassuring me.

"Everyone thinks I have my life in order and I'm on top of things when, in reality, on the inside, I'm a mess. And the older I become, the more afraid and insecure I get."

"What are you afraid of?" he asked.

I shook my head. "Afraid of never feeling in control of my life, of never feeling secure in love, of never finding peace. My life always seems to be haunted by insecurity and doubt. I'm tired of pretending to be something I'm not and never filling the emptiness that lives deep inside me. Charlie," I said, looking at him, "I can't live the lie anymore. Nothing about me seems real, my life seems like an illusion with no real substance. I'm just a big phony who dreams big dreams and accomplishes little. Except for my son and Sarah, I hate my life."

The hopelessness I felt was overwhelming. My next comment brought sadness to the old man's face. "I don't even know if I believe in God anymore. Why would he allow so much pain and sorrow to surround my life? The final straw is I found out just before leaving to come to Montana that I have an incurable eye condition that will leave me blind. Now do you understand why I don't feel thankful or blessed? I have honestly tried to believe and be thankful, but where has it gotten me?" I suddenly realized how good I got at feeling sorry for myself over the years. "What have I done wrong? What is the matter with me?" I asked. "God, please help me. I can't live like this any longer."

Charlie looked at me for a long time before he spoke. "You are much more special than you realize. You have so many wonderful qualities that you have lost sight of, and despite the tragic events that you have encountered on your journey, you have never been alone. God has always been by your side. How else can you explain surviving all that you have and still have a loving and forgiving heart?" The old man's eyes seemed to pierce the depths of my being. Then, in a gentle voice, he expressed his empathy for all that I had laid bare before him. "Ryan, I know you've had many challenges. I know losing your mother at such a young age had a devastating effect on you. Tell me what you remember about her."

I didn't answer immediately. I tried to gather my thoughts and recapture my memories of her. "Charlie," I finally replied, "she has been gone so long and so many of my precious memories of her have disappeared."

"Take your time," he said. "Time has a way of doing that. But there are precious and significant memories that are so important in our lives that we *never* forget. Just tell me about her."

"I remember how beautiful I thought she was. How caring she was, especially for me since I was the youngest. She had a big heart and she cared about people. Charlie, my mom had a rough life growing up, and then with my dad. He wasn't very good to her. When I was around six years old he got into the bar-and-restaurant business so I don't remember him being around much at all. This business led my father down many dark paths. He started having affairs. When I was about seven he bought a business out of town and moved out. At my age I really didn't fully grasp what was going on. My brother and sister, who are significantly older than I am, probably had a better understanding of the destructive impact this had on our family."

A sense of sadness and anger starting to flood over me as the memories of that time returned. Charlie must have sensed the change in my mood. "Go on, son. It's okay. Tell me more."

I continued. "I really felt sad for my mom. She suffered from epilepsy so she couldn't drive and she couldn't work. At that time, the medication couldn't do much to control her seizures which were truly frightening to me as a child. When she would start to have one she would let out this bloodcurdling scream before falling to the floor, gripped by the seizure. She told us she could sense when one was coming because she felt like someone was chasing her. It was awful, especially when she would have one in the middle of the night and it would jolt me out of my sleep. I can remember that I had put together a Superman model kit where he was busting through a brick wall with his fist. For some reason, maybe because I was proud of the job I did on the model, I had put it in her room on her dresser. One night, during her seizure, with her arms flailing, she knocked it off broke it into pieces. I can remember as a little boy joking with her that she was stronger than Superman. I still remember her smiling at my teasing. That's how understanding she was. But there was no humor and nothing funny about what she had to go through. I can only imagine how hopeless and helpless she felt.

"But she was my world. She was the only parent I knew and she loved me. Now, my father kept a roof over our heads and kept us in groceries, but that was about it. My mom was totally dependent on him and at his mercy. She tried to protect me and I don't ever remember her saying a bad word about him. You know, there was a sadness in her that I wanted to make better. I couldn't wait to grow up to get a job and help." The old man kept his eyes on me "She could sing. She was creative and had a beautiful voice. I guess she didn't sing a lot because of her sadness, but I can remember helping her clean the house and hearing her sing as she worked. It was beautiful. We didn't have much of anything and we didn't go away much, only to a few relatives who lived within walking distance. I'm sure her fear of seizures kept her home. A memory sticks in my mind . . . One time she was going out to enjoy herself. I can't exactly remember where she was going, but it was with a lady friend and she got all dressed up. I wasn't used to seeing her like that. She had gone out and got her hair done, something she never did, and she had put on makeup and lipstick. She wore a dark-colored flowered dress and there was a real happiness to her. She was singing and humming while she waited for her friend. I told her she looked like a princess. I was so happy for her." Tears welled in my eyes as I relived the memory. "She deserved a *lifetime* of happiness, not just a few occasions. Why didn't God help her?"

I stopped for a moment as tears streamed down my face. The old man's hand reached out and touched mine. "She sounds like a tough, wonderful woman, Ryan."

"Thank you," I whispered. "You know, anything that is good in me is because of her. In my childish mind I just wanted to be the best little boy I could be and my dream was to grow up and take care of her. It's all I wanted to do and, damn it, God even took *that* from me." Charlie's expression changed at my comment. "I never had my own bike, even at the age of eleven, because my father wouldn't let me. My mother wanted to give me a bike so badly and I found out after she died that she had finally convinced my father to allow me to have one. She was so happy that she was finally going to be able to do this and then she never got the chance.

"I can still remember walking home from school at lunch and my dad opening the door. He always came up on Mondays to do the grocery shopping and I believe this was a Wednesday so he took me by surprise. He sat me down and told me my mother had died. As a little boy, how do you even begin to process that? I don't think I did. I think I just went into shock and the rest is a blur. I remember trying so hard not to cry because I needed to be a big boy.

"I don't think I've ever gotten over that and I guess deep down I've been angry at God ever since." I could see the old man watching me, waiting to see what I would say next. I stood. "Charlie, I try to believe in God, I do, but it's all different now. I mean, the years following her death were a living hell for me. Yes, I'm angry at God.

Over the years I've cursed him, I've raised my fist to him in defiance, and even denied him. My childhood was lost the day she died.

"Why did God take her from me?" I said. "All the special moments I missed with her, and how much I would have loved to have her to turn to in the difficult times. If she hadn't have died I believe my life would have been very different."

Charlie said, "I'm sure that's true. Now you said that anything good in you is because of your mother. Why do you say that?"

"I guess because I do see that I am caring. I can be very loving and forgiving, even in these hard times. These are the qualities I always saw in her." I paused as the memories trickled back. "I can remember my mom telling me that even though we had very little in material things, we always had something far greater and far more special to be thankful for. We had God's love for us. Then she told me all the special qualities that made her who she was were gifts from God, and she was giving them to me and locking them in my heart."

Charlie smiled. "So your mom knew God. Now I'm beginning to understand things even better. Go on.

"We didn't go to church very much but she would talk about God and she would sing praise songs now and then. Charlie, I want to thank you. Many of these memories I thought were gone, they've resurfaced because you made me talk about this. I miss her so much." Then another memory came back to me. "It's really strange, about six months before she died I can remember lying in bed and her coming in to say goodnight. She said, "Ryan my little ray of sunshine, no matter what we go through, and no matter what *you* may go through, God is always with us. You'll never be alone and if you ever find yourself alone or in trouble call out to him, he will take care of you." Then she pulled a small white square from her pocket and unfolded it, revealing two pages. She said she had written a poem just for me. After she read it I felt so special, so loved, and I can remember her smiling at me, giving me a kiss on the cheek, and telling me what a good boy I was, and how proud she was of me." I started to get emotional again but fought back the tears. "I haven't remembered that night in so many years. All these memories are so precious to me." I looked away from him "I lost that poem. What I wouldn't do to have it back.

"I can remember, shortly after she died, how prophetic I thought her words were, but also how comforting.

I can remember imagining her up in heaven with God, looking down over me.

The old man smiled. "I can see in your eyes and hear in your voice how precious these memories are to you. I'm so honored that you shared them with me.

Then a sense of sadness rushed over me as I remembered the reality of that time long ago. "Those words of comfort that my mom gave to me lasted for about six months. I can still remember how lonely I was, how disconnected I felt from my dad, a dad I really didn't know, and soon a stepmother who showed no affection for me at all. My dad was paralyzed in a car accident and my life went from sad and lonely to a living, abusive hell. This is my dilemma, Charlie. I can remember when the abuse and beatings started. I cried out to God and my mom in the midst of my loneliness, in the midst of the horror, and God didn't answer. I knew in my heart that my mother would never lie to me. But at the same time, God never answered me, never rescued me. I can remember thinking so many times, *What did I do to deserve this?* And what kind of God would allow me to go through this when my mom is up there with him?"

I felt as if I were on an emotional rollercoaster, sad one minute, angry another; happy memories, then sad, then around the track again. I was mentally exhausted and I guess the old man could tell. "Ryan," he said, "We've covered a lot. Would you like to take a break?"

"No," I said, "We've come this far, we might as well finish." I took a couple sips from my glass and continued. "The mental and physical abuse continued for years and over that time I lost all hope of God ever rescuing me. It destroyed any self-worth, any self-esteem I had. Hopelessness and the sadness I felt on a daily basis became so overwhelming that I just wanted it to end. I don't know if I've ever shared this with anybody, and it isn't easy, but I just wanted the misery to end." I cast my eyes down to the floor. "There were times I just wanted to end my life and I don't know what stopped me." We sat in silence for several minutes. Part of me wasn't sure what to say next and part of me was shocked by all I shared with this special stranger. And I thought I must have hurt him with the things and feelings I expressed about God. What did he really think of what I said, and how I felt? "Now can you understand why I don't feel very special or why I feel that my life is such a mess? I'm damaged goods. I really am. I thought after all these years I had overcome it but, in baring my soul to you and reliving all this pain I realize all I've done is just buried the hurt and the pain even deeper inside of me. I think I finally understand why certain circumstances trigger all this insecurity and worthlessness to rise up and wreak havoc. And also, if what you say about God is true, how can he ever forgive me?"

Charlie stared into the fireplace for what seemed an eternity, as if he was struggling, searching for the words to answer my question. Finally, he turned to me, emotion swelling in his eyes, and he finally spoke. "I wasn't prepared to get into this tonight, but I know Betsy shared a lot of my story with you. When I lost my daughter and I thought God didn't answer my prayers, nobody was more disappointed or angrier with his God than me. I did all the same things you did. I cursed him, I denied him, I told him I could never follow or believe in a God who wouldn't answer my fervent and continuous prayers. I said, 'Why didn't you save my precious girl? Why, Lord, why?' I acted like this out of emotional distress and out of ignorance of our loving God. In my time of deepest need he reached out and saved me, and when I look back and remember how I treated him, the things I said to him, I was filled with shame. But God loves his children, and we *are* his children, and in his infinite love for us he will also forgive us. He saved me and if you allow him he will save you, too.

"If you say so," I replied somewhat half-heartedly.

"I do say so," he replied. "Remember all those wonderful memories of your mother you shared with me? You told me how kind and forgiving she was, not only to your family, but to others. You said she had such a big heart, that you remember her telling you that she had instilled those same wonderful qualities in you, they were her special gift to you. And she told you that those special qualities in your heart would serve you well. They would guide you to make wise and caring choices in your journey through life. You also said that anything good that was in you was because of your mother. Do you remember that?"

"Yes," I answered, "but why are you bringing this up?"

"Because you have lost sight of the precious gift your loving mother instilled in you. And it's understandable with all the tragic events in your life, the abuse you endured, the pain and heartache of not feeling loved. That resulted in deep-seated insecurity and a lack of trust in people."

"But Charlie, I'm still a loving and caring person. Those qualities are the part of my mother I hold dearly in my heart and I would never lose sight of them," I protested.

But you *have* lost sight of them, at least partially. You have become guarded and measured about expressing and sharing your love. This comes from you hardening your heart to protect yourself from being hurt again. In the process you also hardened your heart to God. This can happen suddenly, especially after a deep loss or hurt, or it can happen gradually, where you don't even realize it until it's too late. This is the main reason behind much of the evil, cruelty, meanness, and corruption in the world today. When people refuse, either in their words or in their actions, to love one another they shut God out of their lives. God's very essence is love. When people harden their hearts to love, the world is in trouble. Where love is absent, hate and evil will fill the void. The devil identifies this weakness and pounces on it. All the destructive evil qualities of the devil pour forth and take root. He will get into your mind and fill it with his deceit, control it with fear and despair and depression and envy and revenge, brutality, even murder. He is running rampant in the world today. He is a masterful liar to keep you, your mind, and your heart turned away from God."

Charlie rose from his chair and stood for a moment, staring at the picture of Jesus above the fireplace. Then he turned to me and smiled. "Go sit at the table. Yes, yes, I think this is the perfect time." he said as he headed towards one of the bookshelves along the wall. As he slid books around on several shelves, as if looking for something, he quietly talked and laughed to himself. He was almost giddy. I sat at the table, watching him, wondering what he was up to. Finally, he said, "Ah, here it is," as he produced something wrapped in well-worn purple satin. He said, "Thank you, Lord. Thank you, Lord," as he sat in the chair across from me and slowly extended his arms toward me with the cloth-covered object in his hand.

"What is this?" I asked.

As I took the object, he said, "This precious gift will open your eyes and your heart to how much God loves you. It will break the hardness around your heart as you witness the truth that anything is possible with God. You told me that you felt a mysterious pull to come out here. That a quiet voice kept telling you to stay true to the path I put you on; trust in me. None of this made any sense to you. It even scared you, but for reasons unknown you made the journey. By doing so you took a giant leap of faith, though I don't think you see it that way. Yes, my son, God has chosen you to be here with me and God has rewarded your faith."

I took the object. My mind was racing. There was no way that this could be from God. I mean, all I knew of God was that he hadn't answered my prayers. And this whole thing about being chosen scared the hell out of me. I mean, who was I? I didn't feel worthy to be chosen nor did I want to be. Any relationship I had with God was damaged and broken. But I did believe and trust this old man. If he said God had something to do with this, I would accept that. I set the object down in front of me, still covered in its cloth. I looked up at Charlie. None of this made any sense to me, and it was freaking me out. I wanted to believe in God like Charlie did, but I didn't. I was filled with a nervous anticipation.

I gently removed the cloth. Sitting before me was a double eight-by-ten carved wooden frame, folded closed and held together by a golden latch. I took several deep breaths. What could possibly be held in these frames that would carry such significance in my quest? Charlie's eyes were fixed on me as I unhooked the latch. I rubbed my fingers slowly across the exquisite frame. Hesitantly, I opened it to reveal its contents. My whole body tingled.

I gasped in disbelief. There, behind the glass, were two handwritten pages. As I read the first few lines my eyes filled with tears and a rush of emotions flooded over me. I felt a great sense of love and gratitude and my heart burst with joy. I peered up at the old man, trying to find the words to say.

He just smiled. Then I noticed the tears. "Charlie, how could you have known? How can this be? My mind questioned the reality of the moment. Was this truly real or was I dreaming? The miracle I held in my hand, was it possible? But I wasn't dreaming. The precious gift in my hands was real.

Enclosed in the frame was the poem my mother had read to me over thirty-one years ago. I could still see the creases in the pages where she had folded them to put in her pocket that night. After she died, I scoured the house and couldn't find them. Maybe my dad had thrown them away. The loss of those pages was one of my life's greatest heartbreaks, and now here they were in my hands.

"Charlie, how do I ever find the words to thank you?"

"It's not me you should be thanking, but God. He deserves all the praise and glory. When the events of this evening finally sink in you will understand the truth. This miraculous gift is from God. He just used me as his vehicle to make it happen. I am so blessed God allowed me to witness his magnificent love for his children. It's glorious to do God's work and be obedient to his purpose for our lives." I realized what he was telling me had to be true, I just couldn't embrace the significance. I was in strange territory. How could any of this be real? How could a stranger know so much about me? But I didn't care. I was just thankful he was there.

"Charlie, how do I turn my life around?" I asked, grabbing his hands.

"You've already started, my son. You've already started."

He pushed his Bible over to me and asked me to read some passages out loud. As I began, he sat back in his chair and closed his eyes. I opened to the first marked passage.

"John 1:1. *In the beginning was the Word and the word was with God and the word was God.*" I turned to the next passage. "John 3:16. *For God so loved the world that He gave His only Son, that whoever believes in Him should not perish, but have eternal life.* John 5:24. *Truly, truly I say unto you, He who hears my words and believes Him who sent Me has eternal life; he does not come into judgment, but has passed from death to life.*" The old man had opened his eyes. They were focused on me. "Acts 2:21." My voice steadied as I proceeded. *"And it shall be that whoever calls on the name of the Lord shall be saved."* The words carried a clarity I had never experienced before. "Ephesians 2:8 and 9. *For by grace you have been saved through faith and this is not your own doing, it is the gift of God, not because of works lest any man should boast.* Romans 10:9 and 10. *Because if you confess with your lips, that Jesus is Lord and believe in your heart that God raised Him from the dead, you will be saved. For man believes with his heart and is so justified and confesses with his lips and so is saved.*" Then I turned to the last marked passage. "John 14:6. *Jesus said to him, 'I am the way, and the truth and the life, no one comes to the Father but by Me.'*"

I will never forget what happened next. I heard that voice. *Stay true to the path I've put you on and trust in me. For I am with you always.* I dropped the book on the table and looked around the room. "Did you hear that?" I asked.

He looked at me, perplexed. "The voice," I repeated. "Did you hear the voice?"

Charlie shook his head and smiled. *I know I heard it,* I thought. I looked at the old man again. I couldn't believe he hadn't heard it.

"Ryan," he finally said. "Do you know why I had you read those passages?"

"I'm not sure," I answered.

"Because first, I want you to know that you are saved by the grace of God, not by the good works you will do. It is God's gift to us that we are saved. Second, that to have a real relationship with God you must accept Jesus Christ into your heart." He looked at me thoughtfully. "Are you ready to ask Christ into your life?"

"Yes," I said. "Yes, I am."

"Then pray to him to come into your life, surrender yourself, your whole self to him, and feel the power of his love."

I lowered my head, closed my eyes, and asked Christ to come into my heart, to breathe new life into my spirit, and to cleanse myself of my old life once and for all. I confessed how much of a mess I had made of my life and that I needed him. As I bared my soul, a strange sensation came over me. At first I felt shame as my past flowed out of me. But then a sensation of freshness, of newness started to build until it filled me with a feeling of love and peace. All the pain and anguish I once felt were gone. I couldn't believe what I was feeling. I said, "Amen" and Charlie greeted me with a smile. I tried to express what I felt, but I couldn't find the words to justly describe them. I never wanted this feeling to end.

Charlie walked over, hugged me, and said he loved me. "Now don't stay up too late," he said. "We have much work to do."

I expected a profound speech or something. Instead, he said goodnight and went to bed.

I wanted to talk and share this experience. How did he expect me to sleep? But I knew better than to try and bring him back. I sat there for the longest time staring into the fire. *What happened here tonight?* I thought. The full understanding of the evening's events were still beyond me. As I sat rocking, bathed in a warm glowing peace, I couldn't comprehend the new life that was about to greet me.

CHAPTER TWENTY-TWO

I awoke just after dawn. The sun was shedding its first light as my senses greeted the new day. I knew something was different. I felt refreshed and new. When I sat up I suddenly realized there was no pain. I crawled out of bed. Nothing. I couldn't believe it. Over the past several weeks I couldn't move or even breathe without pain.

"Thank you, Lord, thank you," I said aloud. "Hallelujah! Hallelujah!" I shouted. I hurriedly dressed. I couldn't wait to share my news with Charlie. Red shared my excitement, barking and running for the door.

Red darted from room to room. I was close behind. "Charlie! Good morning, Charlie! What a wonderful day it is!" I yelled. Suddenly I noticed the silence that filled the cabin. Charlie was always up, humming and whistling. *Where is he?* I thought. God, I wanted to share my feelings with him. Red and I went out on to the porch. I walked around the cabin, but Charlie was nowhere to be found. His pick-up was in the driveway. "Charlie!" I called into the morning air, but there was no response.

Red ran into the woods. I shouted after him. He stopped and turned, acting as if he wanted me to follow him. Maybe he smelled the old man's scent. As I chased after my dog, my thoughts were on Charlie. It wasn't like him to leave and not let me know. He had been there every morning since he took me in. I began to worry. I had been climbing a slight grade for about fifty yards when Red finally stopped about sixty feet in front of me. He just stood there, perfectly still. As I came up beside him, I bent over to catch my breath.

When I looked up, there was Charlie. I rubbed my eyes and shook my head. It was as if I was caught in a dream. Charlie sat on a small log bench in the center of a slight clearing. In front of him was an altar made of stone, maybe twelve to fourteen feet tall with an old wooden cross protruding from the top. The old man's head was bowed in prayer, his forehead resting on his hands. For as long as I live, I will never forget the scene that unfolded before me.

I felt a powerful presence. My skin tingled, I couldn't move. Whatever had a hold on me had a hold on Red, too. He sat perfectly still, not moving a muscle.

The surrounding forest was shedding its coat of darkness, but the clearing where Charlie sat was aglow in light. The sun's rays streaked through the trees, bathing the altar. It was mesmerizing.

I felt like Red and I were intruders. Surely this was a sacred and private place for the old man. After several minutes I decided we should leave and wait for Charlie back at the cabin, but as I turned to go Charlie motioned for me to come and sit next to him. He never looked to see who was there.

I slowly and quietly walked over and sat down next to him. He opened his eyes and smiled. In a soft voice he said, "I didn't know if you'd find me here. Let us pray and give the Lord thanks," he said. I bowed my head and listened to his heartfelt prayer. He gave thanks for all his blessings. He prayed for so many people all over the world that they may come to know God through Jesus Christ. Then he prayed for me. As I sat next to Charlie in prayer, a feeling of serene peace enveloped me to the point of euphoria. The powerful presence bathed us in warmth and love. I felt a true connection with God. Finally, Charlie said, "Amen." I did likewise.

I was numb from the experience and stumbled to regain my balance as I stood. Charlie turned toward me and gave me a long hug. "Bless you, son," he whispered. I tried to speak, but no words came. All I could do was smile at the old man.

The clearing was still aglow. "This, Ryan," he said, spreading his arms. "This clearing is my holy of holies. Here I feel closer to God than anywhere."

We turned and went back to the cabin. "Ryan, when I first came out here, a vision came to me one night and showed that clearing to me. I was instructed to build an altar to God and so I did. I'm so blessed to feel his mercy and witness his awesome glory. His presence and love are all we need in our journey through life."

I longed to share Charlie's deep faith. When he spoke of his love for God, he was always so contented, so at peace.

After breakfast, we read a few passages from the Bible and gave another prayer of thanks. Whatever he asked me to do, I now did without question or hesitation. My trust had firmly been granted to him.

"I'm sure you feel quite different this morning," he said.

"Yes," I said. "The pain in my chest and my head, when I woke up this morning it was gone."

"Oh hallelujah, hallelujah!" he bellowed. "Thank you. Lord, thank you." Then, looking at me seriously, he continued. "Son, the glorious feeling you are experiencing—open yourself up to it. Allow it to grow and flourish inside of you for it is God's love flowing in you. Surrender yourself to its power and beauty for you are in the palms of our loving God. Know and trust that he lives within you, within each one of us, if we will only take the time to be still and to ask. Your new life, your renewed relationship with God, will transform your life if you will allow it. And for your relationship with God to flourish, it must be nurtured in fertile ground. You must communicate with him daily through your thoughts and your prayers. Place your trust and your faith in the knowledge that God loves you. And as a parent only wishes good things for their children, imagine the wonderful things God wants for you."

Charlie's words touched my heart. As my eyes met his, he continued. "You can walk through life never to worry again if only you will carry this faith. If God be for us, who would be against us? Turn all your worries and your problems over to him, for he will lift their burden from your shoulders for all eternity." He looked at me and smiled. "I haven't worried for over forty years, Ryan. Why should I when he gladly takes it from me?"

I shook my head. I had never thought of God in this way before. He is truly on our side, if we will let him be. And then it came to me, the full meaning of Charlie's statement: If God be for us, who would be against us? If I would place my heart and soul in faith with God, who or what could ever harm me, really, with God by my side?

Charlie rose from the table and, in his bellowing voice, said, "It is a glorious day, a glorious day indeed! We have so much to be thankful for, but we also have much work to do before you leave here."

His words struck me hard. I had become so entranced in my experience that I had lost all thoughts of time or of leaving. But I also had no idea what all this work was that he kept talking about. My month was nearly up, but I knew I couldn't leave until we were finished, no matter what the cost. I would ask Charlie to drive me to town tomorrow morning so I could extend my stay. How would everyone react to my desire to stay longer?

CHAPTER TWENTY-THREE

The next morning, after breakfast, Charlie took Red and I on a forty-minute drive to the town of Pines in Charlie's old pickup. Pines was a small town of about six hundred people with a general store, a lumber mill, a tavern and restaurant, and some shops and a garage. This was where Charlie came to stock up.

As we drove through the forest, my mind began to wander. I hadn't been in touch with anyone back home since I left. How would they react to my staying even longer? Would they understand why I needed to?

We finally came to the main road that would lead us to Pines. Charlie turned and, after shifting through the old truck's gears, he looked over and smiled. "You seem rather quiet this morning. A little nervous calling home?" I nodded. The old man must have sensed that I didn't want to talk, and he looked straight ahead, humming as we headed down the road.

I *was* anxious about calling home. There was definitely a change taking place in me. How would I explain it? How could I explain the spiritual and mystical energy of Charlie's Woods? They would all think I had lost my mind in Montana. Still, I had no choice. I couldn't leave, not yet.

We passed the lumber mill just outside of Pines. As we drove down Main Street I watched the townspeople busily going about their business. It felt strange to be out among people after being in Charlie's Woods for the past month.

Everyone knew Charlie. They either called out his name or waved. Red was excited by the activity, too, his tail wagging back and forth. Charlie pointed out the different stores and businesses, telling me about their owners and their history.

He parked in front of the general store. There was a phone booth at the end of the building next to a vacant lot. I climbed out of the truck with Red right behind me. Charlie told me to come into the store. "I want to introduce you to Big Jim," he said. As we walked through the open door it was as if I had stepped back in time. It was dark but clean, with old wood floors and merchandise neatly displayed on the shelves. After my introduction to Big Jim—and believe me, the name fit—Charlie said he had a few people to see. "I'll be back in about twenty minutes or so. Big Jim will let you use his phone. I thought it would be more private than the public phone out front." I thanked him, and he walked out of the store.

Big Jim came around the counter and placed his hand on my shoulder. "Ryan," he said in his deep baritone, "Any friend of Charlie's is a friend of mine. Come on, I'll show you where the phone is." He led me through the back of the store into a small office where he pointed to the phone and a chair. "Make yourself at home," he said, "and just come out when you've finished." I thanked him as he turned to go wait on a customer.

I sat for several minutes wondering who I should call first and what to say. Finally, I took a deep breath and dialed my boss's number. I might as well get this out of the way first. He told me that if I wasn't back by the beginning of the week, he couldn't promise me I would still have my job. "You know I already had to pull strings to get you this leave of absence," he said.

"I know," I answered, "but something's come up and I can't leave yet."

"Do you have any idea when you'll be back?"

"I don't know. It could be several more weeks. I can't give you a definite date."

"The owner isn't going to be very receptive to this and, to be perfectly honest, I don't understand it either. I'll take it to the owner, but I doubt he's going to approve it. We need your territory covered. I'll do what I can." He wished me luck and I thanked him. I couldn't believe it. My first contact with my reality back home and it was a crisis. Man, I couldn't lose my job, but I also couldn't leave here yet. I knew something good was happening to me here, something that would impact the rest of my life. For a moment I felt the fear and anxiety of losing my job. I could imagine the ridicule I would receive if I lost my position because of this trip. People would think I had lost my mind. I could see my ex-wife pouncing on the opportunity to show that I was an unfit and irresponsible father. Reality was back with a vengeance. But then a remarkable thing happened. That voice, I heard it again. *I am with you always, I am the light out of the darkness*. I looked around Big Jim's small office. I was alone. A quiet calm came over me and pushed away the anxiety and fear. I suddenly didn't care what any of these people thought. Something kept telling me it wasn't important.

For the first time in my life I was ready to risk my job for a purpose that I didn't understand. My coming out here and my decision to stay longer were giant steps for me. Though I didn't see it at the time, these were steps of faith.

My next call was to Steve. I talked to him briefly and he assured me everything was fine. He told me to stay as long as necessary, that between him and Sarah they would take care of my house. I asked him how Sarah was doing, and he told me she was fine, but worried sick about me. "She really loves you, Ryan," he said. "I hope you're going to call her."

"I am," I replied, "after I call my son." Steve pressed me for details about my trip. I told him I would explain everything when I got home, but that he might not recognize his best friend. Again, he wished me luck.

"Dad, is that you?" the boyish little voice said through the phone. I couldn't hold back my tears of joy in hearing it. The impact of how much I missed him hit hard. "When are you coming home?" he asked. I told him how much I loved him and how much I missed him. I searched for the words to explain that I wouldn't be coming home for a while yet.

"Daddy needs to take care of some business before I come home," I said, "but I promise I'll be home as soon as I can, probably in a couple of weeks." The disappointment in his voice broke my heart. Again, I told him how much I loved him and to put his mom on the phone so I could tell her my plans. She said it was fine with her and there was no problem keeping Brent, but I could also hear the antagonism in her voice. I was sure she wondered what I was up to.

I took several deep breaths before I called Sarah. I realized now why I saved her for last. Calling her stirred the most fear and anxiety. Though I was calm in my decision to stay, I wondered how she would react. Was Steve right that she still loved me or was I testing her patience to the breaking point? And how would she feel about me staying longer at the risk of losing my job? Would she think I had gone crazy?

My stomach knotted as I heard the buzzing ringtone. "Hello," came her soft angelic voice. At first I couldn't speak. "Hello?" she said again.

"Sarah," I said hesitantly.

"Ryan, is that you?" Her excitement was unmistakable. "How are you? Are you okay? I've been so worried about you."

"I'm fine, Sarah. Really, I'm fine."

"Somebody named Charlie called and said you had been beaten. I've been so worried, even though he assured me you would be fine. Oh, Ryan, I've missed you so much." And then she broke down and started to cry. I felt awful for not calling her sooner. I realized what I must have put her through, all this time away without a word.

"I'm sorry, Ryan. I didn't mean to cry, but I'm so happy to hear your voice. I love you so much." Her voice was filled with emotion.

"I love you too, and I'm so sorry to put you through all of this. Please don't cry."

"I'm just so happy and relieved," she said, regaining her composure. "Did you find your answers? Where are you anyway? When are you coming home?"

"Slow down," I said. "I can only answer one question at a time." I heard her laugh. "Thank you, Lord," I said.

"I want to feel your arms around me again. How soon will you be home?"

"That's part of the reason I'm calling. I need to stay awhile longer."

"Longer? How much longer?"

"Several weeks, but I'm not exactly sure. And I might have lost my job, too." She was silent.

"Ryan, what's going on? You're being mysterious. Are you sure about this?"

"Yes, I am. I can't explain everything on the phone. When you said you believed God was behind the pull I felt to come out here, I wasn't convinced. But now I know it's true." I assured her that I knew without a doubt that I was where I was supposed to be and that the answers I sought would be found here. I just hoped she'd recognize me when I got home. I told her about Charlie, which triggered a thousand more questions.

I promised her that I would call her as soon as I was ready to head back. "I know this probably doesn't make a lot of sense, but just trust me on this. Your love and understanding mean more to me than you can know. Something good, something amazing is happening here and that's why I can't leave yet. I must see this through. It means so much that you're still there for me."

"I will always be here for you," she said softly. "Never forget that." Her words stuck in my heart. I sat for the longest time just holding the telephone receiver in my hand. I felt a sudden urge to pray.

I bowed my head and asked the Lord to forgive me for my past whining and complaining. These phone calls made me realize how blessed I was. I knew in my heart that I had more riches than any king and that I had blinded myself to the true blessings God had given me.

I thanked Big Jim for the use of his phone and asked what I owed him. He smiled, shook my hand, and said, "Charlie has already taken care of it."

I looked out the store window and there sat the old man, waving to me from his truck. I opened the truck door and motioned for Red to jump in and I followed him. Charlie turned the key and the motor roared to life. He pointed to the horizon. "There's a storm coming. Let's try to get home before it gets too bad. Everything okay back home?" he asked before pulling away.

"Everything's fine. At least I think so. They probably all think I'm crazy."

"Nothing to be concerned about," he said. "Some people think I'm crazy, too."

As we drove down the highway, I shared my phone conversations. I told him how blessed I felt to have such a wonderful woman as Sarah. "She loves you very much, I can tell," he said. "And what a wonderful son you have."

"I know, and it broke my heart to tell him I wasn't coming home right away. I miss him."

I also shared how thankful I was to Sarah and Steve for taking care of my home and garden while I was here.

"Do you feel its power?" Charlie asked.

"What power?"

"The power of being thankful. Think how good you feel right now. That is the wonder, the gift of being thankful for your blessings. Now do you see why I give thanks every day?" I nodded and smiled. *He certainly is a wise man,* I thought. It did feel good to be happy.

"And what about your work?" Charlie asked. "Were they understanding?"

I shook my head. "I don't know. I don't have a good feeling about it. I'll probably lose my job."

He turned off the main road onto the forest lane, then he pulled over and stopped the truck. "And how do you feel about that, son?" he asked.

"At first I was filled with anxiety and fear," I replied. "But then a sense of calm came over me and I heard the voice I heard the other night. Charlie, I can't leave until it's finished."

"Good," he said. "You're learning to listen." He placed his giant hand on mine. "God doesn't give bad advice. Remember today, because today you passed a big test of faith. Remember, God is on your side. He will take care of you." A big grin spread across his face as he put the truck in gear and stepped on the gas.

As we turned on the road that led to Charlie's home, the storm that we'd been skirting finally let loose. Claps of thunder and streaks of lightening filled the sky. Raindrops plopped on the windshield and grew in intensity.

I watched Charlie drive as the storm bore down. "Beautiful, just beautiful," he said. He whistled and hummed as we bounced down the road. Love and peace and gratitude for life emanated from this kind and wonderful old man. I could feel it whenever I was in his presence. I leaned my head back against the seat and closed my eyes.

My thoughts turned to my phone conversations. Charlie said I had passed a test of faith, but had I? Now a small part of me questioned my decision to stay at the risk of my job. I never would have made such a risky decision before. Something about me had changed, there was no doubting that. The embers of doubt inside me were flaring up again. I wondered if part of what I would find here was the deep unshakable faith and sacred peace that Charlie had found. God, I hoped so.

CHAPTER TWENTY-FOUR

The sky was clear, the storm had gone. After a simple lunch we sat on the porch to enjoy the clearing skies. "Charlie, when I came out here I was surely a lost and, I see now, ungrateful soul. Today, when I made those phone calls, I realized how blessed I am. Why, then, am I still so confused? And what about risking my job, isn't that irresponsible? And everything that's happening to me, I don't know what it all means."

"Whoa, whoa, one question at time," he responded. "Now, first of all, you're starting to worry again. Worry serves no positive purpose, that's why God tells us to turn our worries over to him. And, son, that takes faith. Old habits are hard to break and that's part of what you're experiencing. Faith, like trust, needs to be worked at. It won't come overnight.

"Faith is an all-or-nothing deal," he continued. "You either have it or you don't. You can't say *I have a little faith,* because that is a contradiction. Complete faith means having no doubts. Total faith is the only way to have a deep personal relationship with God.

"It's one of the major problems in our world today. Too many people worry too much. They worry about things that, more often than not, never become reality. They allow their worries to slowly suffocate the life right out of them until they're filled only with worry. And their constant worries turn into fear and bitterness and attract a host of other negative forces—jealousy, low self-esteem, and blame. They soon convince themselves that all their misfortunes are someone else's fault, totally shirking any responsibility for their own despair, for their own choices. Why do you think Jesus tells us in the Bible that worry is a sin? He does so because worry produces nothing positive. It's not even real. This is part of the work we need to do. To practice the act of faith daily. To break your old thought habits and realize the power of absolute faith in our loving God will remove worry from your life forever."

His words were powerful and I hungered for more. "Ryan," he continued, "everything you are feeling and thinking is normal. You have just started to experience a new revelation of God's love through Christ. The feeling is euphoric and beautiful. You feel peace and love as you have never felt before. You want to hold it tightly and never let go. But then the events and feelings and experiences, all that makes you who you are today, try to come back and pull you down. Your human nature wants to return to its comfort zone, no matter how much misery and despair comes along with it."

"But why? I mean, to hear you say that, well, it doesn't make any sense."

"No, it doesn't. But in God's infinite wisdom, he knew that for us to truly experience the purity of his love we must, by our own choice, choose to go to him. God knew that the true wonder of his creation would never be realized if we were *forced* to love him. Oh, Ryan, the heartache he must feel by the many choices we make! But by his precious gift of free will, which he gives to all of us, he also reveals his true unselfish and unconditional love. This is a perfect love which is impossible for us to experience with another human being. Think about it. All your life you have witnessed, at least in your own perception, conditional love."

"That's not true," I protested.

"I never said it was necessarily *true,* only that it was our perception. As a child, do you feel your parents love you more when you're good or bad? As a child, we relate to this ideal. It's our motivation to be good and to please our parents. When do they shower us with loving praise? When we're good, right? Now don't get me wrong, our parents love us, and we love our children and our spouses. But the way we have learned to *express* our love is usually conditionally.

"Now what comes along with this perception of conditional love is that when we displease and anger, when we hurt the ones we love, we begin to form the perception that we do not deserve, or we're unworthy of, their love. Now, granted, this is only a perception because real love is unconditional, but when we start to feel unworthy or unloved, then the seeds of evil have found a place to grow."

His words gave me new insight to my own feelings and experiences. He stood up and walked to the edge of the porch, then turned and looked at me thoughtfully. His next words bowled me over. He answered my questions before I could ask them. "This is why you feel unworthy of Sarah's love. This is why you create such a struggle, such a crisis in your life by not allowing yourself to commit your love to her."

I shook my head. "I don't know how you know what you know," I said, "but you are right. I've been grappling with that question since I talked to her today." I walked to the edge of the porch next to Charlie and stared out through the trees. "What do I do about it? I certainly don't want to hurt her."

"I know you don't," he replied. "Open your heart and allow her love to flow in unconditionally. Erase any false perceptions you may have, because they are not *hers*. She loves you for who you are, your good qualities and your faults. Allow her love to help strengthen and inspire you, to complete you. I know a true love like hers is new to you. And when we experience something powerful and new in our lives we rush to find an explanation for it, to define it."

We walked inside and he motioned for me to sit at the table. He opened his arms to the rows of books that filled the room. "Here in all these millions and millions of beautiful words written by these wonderful authors are the lessons of life and the secrets of happiness. God gave us the wonder of communication with each other. No other creature has the creative freedom or ability to communicate as we do. In all these thousands and thousands of books are creative and passionate writers who wish to reach out to their fellow man and share the magnificent adventure we call life. Some wish to share life's good fortunes, others share valuable life lessons learned from heartache and despair. Others wish to inspire us to reach for the stars. Still others try to explain the meaning of life and our purpose in it. So much can be learned by picking up a good book and reading it. Books helped change my life and I've been reading steadily ever since. This is why I call this my *Library of Life*."

I wondered how anyone could ever read so many books. "Yes, I've read nearly every one of these," he said. I swore he could read my thoughts. "But one book in particular means more to me than all the others." He uncovered his Bible and clutched it to his chest, holding it close as a mother would a child.

"Forty-two years ago a dear lady gave me this book, shortly after I almost took my life."

Charlie noticed my look of surprise.

"I know Betsy shared my story with you. It's why you have so many questions about me." I smiled and shook my head. "I was sitting in Central Park alone, trying to understand the meaning of the visions I had witnessed. I had a new thirst for life because I knew my wife and daughter were at peace in Heaven. But still, the voice saying I had work to do mystified me. Then a kindly lady sat down next to me on the park bench. We exchanged helloes and chatted for a while. She told me she sensed my turmoil and my need of help to find my way out of the darkness. I was stunned by her forwardness but amazed by her accuracy. She reached into her bag and pulled out this book." He patted his Bible.

"She offered it to me and, as I took it from her, she touched my hand. I can still remember the warmth and comfort that passed between us. I told her I already owned several Bibles. She just smiled. 'Please,' she said, 'I want you to have this one.' She got up to leave and made one last comment. 'Open your heart and love your fellow man, for we are all children of God. Walk in faith.' Then she walked away. I sat there holding her Bible when I noticed how beautiful and unique her gift was. I had never seen a Bible like it. I couldn't keep such an exquisite gift from a stranger, so I ran after her. She was nowhere in sight. It was as if she had vanished. I tucked the book inside my coat and walked home. I gave it no more

thought until after I sat down with a cup of tea before re-
tiring for the night. There, on the table, sat the Bible she
gave me. I found myself continuously looking at it as if
guided by some unseen force. Finally, I went over and
picked it up. I noticed how soft its leather cover felt in my
hands, and the more I looked at it the more I appreciated
what a fine Bible it was. The cover had been hand-crafted,
the leatherwork was truly exquisite. The edges of the
pages sparkled as if they were trimmed in real gold. I
opened the cover and found these words written inside . . ."

*Dear Charlie, in these pages are the secrets to a
joyous and fulfilling life. To uncover their secrets these
pages must be studied, not just read. Each day—morning
and evening—study a few chapters and soon the secrets
will reveal themselves to you. But first, study the passages
I have outlined. They will open the door to a new and
wonderful life. Surrender yourself to their meaning and
ask Christ to come into your heart. You will experience a
glorious rebirth. Always remember that we are joyous
blessings of God and His love is the eternal flame of hope
that burns in our hearts. Know He is always with you, in
good times and bad, and take absolute comfort in that
knowledge. You have been chosen, yes, chosen to share*

His message of love and hope with those in need. The Lord will guide you on your journey. Take time to be still and pray to Him. In time, another will be sent to you, lost in his own confusion, struggling to escape the darkness of his own making. He will be chosen too, for he has been blessed with a gift that his own turmoil has blinded him from seeing. You will help him see and you will pass this treasured text on to him, a new generation to carry God's message to the world. Take joy in living, and experience your days in thankfulness.

His eyes were wet with tears as he closed the book. He looked at me. "It was addressed to me, Charlie. But I never told her my name. And there was no signature," he said, "but the profound impact she had on my life lives on till this day.

"You see, forty-two years ago I completely surrendered myself to the Lord and accepted Jesus Christ into my heart, just as you did the other evening. The lady who gave me this Bible had marked the same passages that I had you read, so when I promise you a new life in God, I'm talking from experience. God led me to this wilderness and here I settled. Wealth no longer carried the importance in my life that it once had. After buying this property, I donated much of my money to missionaries and charities, keeping enough to help those in need, like yourself, and to take care of my basic needs. I've never felt happier or more fulfilled in my life."

I was awestruck by his story, his honesty, and his openness. He wrapped his sacred Bible back in its cover.

"But Charlie," I said, "why am I really here? Why would I be chosen to come out here and meet you? I'm nobody to be chosen; I'm not worthy of all this."

"Oh, but you are. We are all God's children, and he must have something very special in mind for you."

I just stared. I was totally dumbfounded and confused by his last statement. This was all too bizarre for me to comprehend. Charlie must have noticed my confusion. "Be patient. Your answers will come soon, just be patient."

We got up and walked outside. The storm was long gone and there was a freshness in the air. "Glorious, isn't it?" Charlie said as he took a deep breath of the clean fresh air.

Charlie said he had some chores to do. I offered to help, but he told me to take time to think over what we had just discussed. "Clear your mind and just listen to your thoughts, really listen to them, for in them you will recognize God's voice."

I took a walk, but I couldn't empty my mind. So much had transpired this day, along with all the emotions of calling back home. I tried not worrying about my job, but how could I not? And this wise old man telling me I was chosen to be here—there was no way I could clear my mind of all these thoughts.

Later that night I tossed and turned in bed. All kinds of thoughts filled my mind. What was going to really happen here and what lay ahead for me? I wondered if forty-two years ago Did Charlie struggle with the knowledge of being mysteriously chosen as I did now? I would barely sleep at all that night.

CHAPTER TWENTY-FIVE

Over the next several weeks I was both honored by and blessed with Charlie's teachings. We discussed religion, philosophy, self-improvement, and spiritual growth.

We took long walks through his majestic woods, embracing the incredible beauty of God's creation. I was amazed by the incredible joy the old man got from the simple pleasures of life. He could be like a child seeing a butterfly or a beautiful flower for the first time. His living example gave me an appreciation for life that I hadn't felt before.

Twice daily, morning and evening, time was set aside for our spiritual relationship with God. Charlie derived so much pleasure from this.

Each morning after breakfast we would visit his altar and pray. Then, back at the cabin, we would study passages from the Bible. One morning, before we started

to read, Charlie held his Bible up and said, "So many people see the Bible has merely a book containing pages of
words. They think it was written by men and not by God.
Because they have this perception they get little or nothing out of it. This explains while so many Bibles sit on
shelves collecting dust."

As I listened I realized that *was* how I viewed the
Bible. Charlie continued. "I, too, once saw the Bible that
way. But one glorious morning the Holy Spirit revealed
to me the truth about God's word. The Bible is *God
breathed*, which means the Holy Spirit was upon all those
involved in writing it. God's spirit guided every printed
word. This is why God's word is living and powerful. The
Bible contains the very essence of God. Ryan, this is why
I have such a deep love and reverence for God's word.
When I hold the Bible lovingly to my chest I hold the very
essence of God. Do you comprehend this magnificent
truth?"

I was awestruck. As the presence of God's spirit
washed over me, I was enveloped in a depth of understanding that I had never known before. Still shaken, I finally answered him. "I do, I really do," I exclaimed. We
spontaneously fell to our knees by the table, praising God.

With each day my new spirit grew and blossomed under Charlie's watchful and caring eye. Our daily reading of God's word took on a profound and deeper meaning for me. A new, vibrant inner strength was replacing my old fears and insecurities. Peace, love, and compassion were now a living part of me, all because of God's love flowing through me.

One afternoon, as we were on one of our daily walks, Charlie said he wanted to share a special place with me. We had been walking a half hour or so when I saw a clearing up ahead. As we got closer to it Charlie slowed his pace. "Out there," he said, pointing to the clearing, "is one of God's masterpieces. I'm so filled with joy that I can share this with you, Ryan. This is one of my favorite places to visit on all the Earth." The old man truly had my curiosity going, because from here I couldn't understand his exuberance. He smiled and we continued on. When we reached the clearing, the afternoon sun bathed our faces in warmth. We stopped to catch our breath. I was mystified by Charlie's stamina, for he was nearly twice my age and there were times when I could barely keep up with him. We walked a little farther to the top of the knoll. A spectacular scene unfolded before us. A meadow filled with a spectacular array of wildflowers gently swaying in the breeze. In the distance, a herd of deer grazed, stopping their eating momentarily to check us out. Charlie pointed to the sky where a pair of bald eagles soared high above us. Butterflies danced from flower to flower and the sounds of birdsong filled the air. On the horizon were snow-covered mountain peaks. The old man turned to me, a giant grin on his face. "Isn't this just glorious?"

"Yes," I replied. "It's beautiful."

Then he continued walking ahead of me. He stopped after about fifty yards. He yelled for me to join him. As I approached I heard the rush of water. Where was it was coming from? When I was nearly even with him I realized that he stood at the edge of a gorge which had been hidden by the tall meadow grass. A spectacular waterfall on the other side dropped into the gorge, at least a hundred and fifty feet to the bottom. Everything around us was so fresh, so clean. The sheer grandeur of this place was stunning. The kaleidoscope of sight and sound filled my senses with euphoria.

"This is quite a masterpiece," I finally said.

"Every time I come here it's like the first time. Everything is so alive. Nature beating in harmonious perfection. Can you feel the peace and tranquility that surround us?"

"Yes, I can."

He raised his arms to the sky and shouted in his bellowing voice, "Oh, thank you, Lord. Thank you for this beautiful place!"

Then he was more serious. "Ryan, I pray that the state of Montana honors my wishes and never allows anyone to compromise the beauty that surrounds us here. Let's sit and rest a spell."

"Okay," I said.

"Whenever I slip a little, or start to take for granted the precious gift of life, I come here to regain my perspective on the beauty of it all. People are in such a rush these days. They remind me of ants scurrying about their duties, never taking time to appreciate the treasures that surround them. They exercise their bodies and their minds, but totally neglect their spiritual connection to God. They scurry about at a dizzying pace so they can possess more material wealth, but the more they possess, the more they want. Happiness and contentment are always just another possession away. Suddenly they are old and their constant pursuit of more has left them tired and empty.

"The sad part is they always had choices. Oh, what a dangerous gift God gave us, *choice*." He squeezed his thumb and forefinger together and then parted them slightly. "If they would only take a tiny bit of their time each day to be still and allow their inner voice to speak, to nurture their spirit, to hear God's voice, they would experience a life greater than they have ever known. But people convince themselves they can't afford to take time for themselves. Others are afraid of facing their inner voice, for they know the life they live is out of control and morally empty. In their arrogance and ignorance they try to convince themselves that only they can get themselves out of the mess they've made of their lives. If they would just take time and be still. What a pity."

I nodded my head in agreement, marveling at the simplicity of his wisdom.

"Often when I come here I take time to pray and give thanks to God and become one with the beauty around me. Now close your eyes and take slow, deep breaths. Slowly clear your mind of all thoughts until there is only one voice, one source of thought. Allow yourself to feel total peace. Breathe in the beauty that is all around you, lose yourself in its majesty. When your mind is clear, be still and listen. His voice will be your thought. Give it total freedom, for in your stillness will come the answers you seek."

At first it seemed torturous to sit still for more than ten minutes, but the more we meditated the more natural it became. Meditation, like my daily prayer time, became a spiritual connection to God.

As I sat with my eyes closed in this majestic setting, I felt the harmonious rhythm of God's creation. With my mind clear I became aware of God's presence. Suddenly, I was filled with the understanding of how connected all of us really are, and if we would just listen to his commandment, each one of us could help the world. The voice was so real. *Love one another as I have loved you.* I didn't want to leave this place. I felt so loved, so at peace.

Charlie slowly rose to his feet, distracting me out from my meditative state. It took me several minutes to regain my senses. He put his big arm around me as we started our hike home.

"So," he said, "there is hope. Yes, there is real hope for the world, but God needs many messengers to touch people's hearts and souls. You're to be one of his messengers, Ryan."

I stopped walking and stared at him. He laughed. "What's the matter?"

"What did you just say?"

He laughed again. "You're to be a messenger of hope and inspiration."

"How? Why? How?" I asked. "How can I inspire anyone else?"

He touched my shoulder. "Ryan, the answer will come to you before you leave here. Be patient and listen."

One truth was becoming clear. God's plan is not always *our* plan. Though it still wasn't clear how, I knew that I would leave this place a very different man.

CHAPTER TWENTY-SIX

The next morning, after breakfast, I sat rocking on the porch. I still could not believe all that had happened to me since my arrival. Day by day, week by week, a new and very different me was being created. The only way for me to even try to explain the change in me was, well, I was changing from the inside out. My new spirit was emerging from deep in my soul. I was beginning to understand, to *really* comprehend the message, *Ye must be born again.* These words precisely described what was happening to me. Slowly, like a new baby emerging from his mother's womb, the new man in me was being given new life.

At first I wasn't aware of the changes, but day by day my new life was being nurtured and refreshed by our loving God.

Nearly two months had passed and my whole perspective on life had been drastically altered. Our daily praying, our daily giving of thanks, our daily reading of God's word all were molding me into a new man. Yes, it really was a rebirth.

As I sat there rocking, reflecting on my time here, I felt so blessed. I had never felt so at peace with who I was, or so loved, as I did now. My feelings of insecurity, of failure, had all disappeared. As my thoughts turned to all the people in my life, they all took on a new appearance. I felt only thankfulness for those who were close to me. I felt a new depth of love and compassion. I now knew that Sarah being in my life was orchestrated by God, and instead of fearing her love, I eagerly embraced it. I never thought it was possible to love my son more than I did, but even that was made clearer by God. I had new insights and new purpose in being a father.

To those in my life I didn't feel close to before, or even like, I now cast no judgment. I realized that all my negative and destructive thoughts had vanished—they were gone, buried. I stood up, straight and tall, filling my lungs with the clear crisp air, thrusting my chest out, then slowly exhaling. The very revelation of the new man living inside me was overwhelming. The sheer joy I felt I can't find the words to describe!

How, you ask, can such a transformation be possible? Only one way: by the grace and love of God flowing through me as living water through this special and kind old man named Charlie, by the sheer power of love, true, unconditional love. I could envision, as I stood there lost in my thoughts, the very transformation of mankind if we would honor Christ's last commandment: *Love one another, as I have loved you.* The impact of the understanding of this simple truth jolted me. Now I clearly understood our connection to one another. Our feeling of insignificance is demolished by this truth. We are responsible for each other. Our actions, our feelings are truly significant to each other. I felt as if God were giving me a small glimpse of his glory. I felt woozy from my experience and sat back down.

The old man appeared on the porch. I buried my head in my hands. "Thank you, Lord, thank you," I said. I looked up, shaking my head. Charlie smiled. "Charlie," I said, my voice quivering, "Would you please sit down?" I slowly shared my experience and my thoughts. He listened intently, nodding his head. When I finished, he sat quietly for a moment, studying me. Then he closed his eyes and I heard him softly say, "Thank you, Lord. Thank you, sweet Jesus. Oh, Ryan, how his spirit has grown in you these past months. What a blessing it is for me to witness the spirit of God in you. God bless you, son, God bless you."

I felt very special in Charlie's presence. How could I ever thank him for saving my life? That's really what he had done. In two short months, he had become a significant part of my life, he had become my mentor. I so cared for and admired him. His gift of love was beyond measure. I watched him as he rocked in his chair, that look of serene peace that was truly part of him.

All his joy came from serving God. His deep faith opened God's kingdom to him. His commitment to helping his fellow man was true and pure. The love and power of Christ flowed out of him.

"Charlie, I just want you to know that I love you and I'm eternally grateful for you in my life."

He smiled and replied, "I love you too, son."

We stood up and embraced each other.

After lunch we walked to Charlie's special place. On our way he said this was a very special day and we would have a celebration dinner this evening.

"What are we celebrating?" I asked.

"I'll tell you this evening," he replied. As we reached the clearing the magnificent beauty of this place took my breath away once again. A powerful divine presence filled Charlie's Woods, but especially so at his altar and here. It filled me with a deep feeling of belonging, of peace and of love. This powerful presence, which once was mysterious and somewhat frightening, no longer was. I, filled with the spirit of Christ, was a new man with new eyes to see.

We sat in our usual spot and reveled in the beauty that surrounded us. Charlie gave a prayer of thanks and then we meditated for over an hour.

My visions returned. I was speaking before large groups of people, sharing the gift of our salvation in Christ, and God's glory in us learning to love one another. I was totally consumed by the experience. When I finished my meditation, I shared the experience with Charlie. "What does this all mean?" I asked.

"Oh, ye of little faith," he said. "Did I not tell you that you are special, that you have been blessed with a gift?"

261

"But what gift? I still don't understand."

"You will," he replied. "Be patient."

That evening Charlie put together a very special dinner—fresh brook trout that he himself had caught earlier that morning, and new potatoes and fresh vegetables from Betsy's garden. We cooked outside over an open fire, the air filled with the heavenly aroma of our meal. It reminded me of camping trips with Sarah. I missed her and couldn't wait to wrap her in my arms again.

"You'll have good news for her soon," Charlie said. He loved teasing me like this.

"Who will I have good news for?" I asked.

"That beautiful lady of yours."

"How . . . oh, never mind," I said, shaking my head. He never admitted that he knew my thoughts, but what other explanation was there? "What news will I have to tell her?" I asked.

"We'll talk after dinner," he said with a chuckle. I resigned myself that he would tell me when he was ready.

We ate slowly, savoring each and every bite. I can't remember ever enjoying a meal more that I did that one. Everything was delicious and Betsy's homemade bread was a treat.

"I can't eat another bite," I said, leaning back in my chair.

The old man smiled. "I'm glad you enjoyed it."

The evening sun cast a parade of shadows among the trees. The sounds of life sprung up around us as various animals and birds busied themselves to feed.

Charlie poured us each a cup of tea. We sat back, observing the beauty that surrounded us. I was convinced that God put glimpses of Heaven on Earth to stir our imaginations to the sheer glory of his creation.

"Ryan," Charlie said, his voice sincere and purposeful, "you have grown in so many ways since we first met. You've been a wonderful student and a treasured friend. Someday you, too, will experience the joy I feel now, the total joy of witnessing God's love, his spirit marrying itself to a person's heart. Like a flower bursting into bloom, its beauty radiates for all to see. In two short months I have witnessed the rebirth of your spirit and watched your inner self be transformed. I've seen a young man filled with fear and doubt blossom into a man filled with the strength and confidence of his new faith and love of God. You have come a long way. Never doubt that God knew the turmoil you were in. That's why he kept tugging at your spirit until you did something crazier than anything you've ever done before: You came out here without even knowing why. A journey into the unknown, a journey that will make some back home question your very sanity. You didn't realize it at the time, but you came out here on faith—blind faith. Remember, everything in life happens for a purpose. Unfortunately, many people ignore the circumstances in their lives and they too often shrug off important crossroads as coincidences."

The old man looked at me with a solemnity I hadn't seen before. "Hear me when I say there are no coincidences. Everything, every person we meet, every circumstance that passes through our lives, has a purpose. Many times it's God's way of communicating with us, guiding us. The secret to joy and peace is to pay attention to the events in our lives, no matter how small. God orchestrates the people and events that come into our lives so he can mold us to his purpose. He is trying to direct us to our destiny. And if we'll take time to talk to him, ask him what we're to learn from these meetings, these circumstances, he'll give us the answers. The Holy Spirit will provide us with clarity and understanding and will guide us into all truth. This is why it's imperative that we spend time daily in prayer with God and immerse ourselves in God's word.

"Son," he said, looking into my eyes, "I have come into your life for a reason, and you into mine. Now, we could be like many people and ignore our chance meeting, or we can accept the fact that we were brought together for his purpose. Do you understand what I'm saying?" His words were profound. And I understood their meaning.

"Yes, Charlie," I answered. "There were times after I first arrived that I just wanted to leave. I was scared by the mystery of all this, and you. But a voice inside me kept telling me to stay and, through our time together in prayer, and our discussions, I knew I couldn't leave. I didn't understand, but deep down I knew God brought me here."

"Oh, bless you, bless you," he said, his voice rising. "That is the power of faith. Never forget this, Ryan. Faith in him is everything, and God's word tells us that he is a rewarder of faith to those who diligently seek him. The peace and joy you witness in me is founded in my undying faith and trust in my Heavenly Father. I don't know where he's taking me much of the time, but I always know that he loves me and watches over me." He laughed and shook his head. "People make life so complicated and they look for the answers in all the wrong places. All my wealth and material possessions never gave me a minuscule of the peace and joy that is part of me now. *That* I owe to my relationship with God. Remember these truths, Ryan," he continued. "God never give us more than we can handle, and in him is all, all we ever need. Carry these truths with you in life and worry will no longer exist." His words stirred my heart and carried a clarity of meaning deeper than I knew before.

"Then why is there so much suffering and evil in the world?" I asked. "Why do we choose to go down a darker road? I mean, what makes people do and act the way they do?"

He looked over his glasses with a hint of sadness. "Because we are all born into this world as sinners, all of us. It's in our nature to be sinners, to be desirous of earthly things, things of the flesh. It's in our make-up. God knew when he gave us freedom of choice that a new reality came with it. Life is the way it is because it is. Do you understand that?"

"I'm not sure," I answered. "you make it sound too simplistic."

He thought for a moment. "Look at it this way. How could you experience joy without knowing sadness? How could you experience health and healing without knowing sickness and disease? How could you experience love without knowing hate? Life is the way it is." This last statement he emphasized slowly and deliberately. "God knew that for us to experience the beauty of life, to embrace and savor the feelings and emotions of love and kindness and compassion, all those glorious gifts of God, we had to be aware of their opposites."

To my surprise, it was making sense. Like a light going off, I sensed an understanding of God's brilliance in his creation.

Charlie stood and continued. "Understanding comes when we quit putting so much energy into questioning *why*, and start just believing. Faith brings understanding. One of the things Jesus witnessed during his short stay on Earth was the weakness of our human nature. This is why he proclaimed, *Fear not the world, for I have overcome the world.* By the power of his faith and love for his Heavenly Father he overcame the weaknesses of human nature. It's that precious and powerful gift God graces each and every one of us with. By trusting and loving him, he will provide us all that we ever need to overcome the world. Yes, by a simple choice of worshipping our Heavenly Father, by placing our trust and faith in him, life on this planet, our relationships with one another, would be gloriously transformed." The old man's voice was filled with excitement.

"Love, Ryan, is the most powerful force on Earth. Do you know why?" He continued before I could answer. "Because love is the very essence of God. When we feel love we are experiencing him. That's how great his love really is. Love is our direct connection to God. In each of us he gave our hearts the ability to love without end. Do you hear that? Our hearts have the capacity to love without limit. Oh, what a glorious, glorious gift he gave us. Can you even imagine the sheer glory of realizing our hearts have no bounds in their ability to love? He raised his hands in the air. "Thank you, Lord, thank you."

Never had I heard Charlie speak with such conviction. He sat back down and smiled. "Love," he said, "is a beautiful and precious gift from God. We all should give of it more freely."

He took a few deep breaths and continued. "When problems and turmoil come into our lives, don't shrink from them in fear, but have faith in the knowledge that our problems are gifts from God in disguise."

"That's hard to accept," I said under my voice.

"Think back and reflect on your life and those around you. Are we not strengthened by adversity? Do we not show compassion and love in crisis? Our greatest spiritual growth often comes during times of crisis and turmoil. That is when God reveals that in him is all we ever need." I thought of my grandmother who was blind for most of her adult life. She lived her life filled with more joy and peace than any of us with sight. I don't think I remember her ever complaining about anything. She celebrated her life with the love of God and Christ. She always praised him. I smiled thinking back at how happy she was. I didn't appreciate the power of her faith in God as a child, but the impact was hitting me now. How I wished I would have taken the time as an adult to spend more time with her and allowed her to share her joy in Christ with me. I had always been too busy to spend time with her. In many ways she reminded me of Charlie, for she, too, had that inner peace and joy. The loss and missed opportunity brought me to tears.

"What is it?" he asked.

"Oh, nothing. I was just thinking of my grand-mother and the joy and peace that were part of her because of her love and faith in God."

The old man smiled. "Ryan, we witness the glory of his love in peoples' lives every day. Every day we hear of miracles, witness the wondrous transformation of the human spirit, yet people still doubt and don't believe. They of little faith, how sad," he said, shaking his head.

"Charlie," I said, still filled with emotion. "Will I have the strength and courage that she had when I lose my sight?" A strange calmness settled over me as I spoke those words. When I received news of my eye disorder, of having RP, and that it would slowly rob me of my sight, it shook me to my very core. It had been the event that pushed me over the edge and led to my decision to come here. But now I was enveloped in a quiet calm. How different I felt.

Charlie gently put his hands on mine. Looking into my eyes, he spoke softly. "Son, I know how devastating it was for you getting the news about your eyes. Remember what I told you. The events in our lives and their timing are always for a reason, for God's purpose. I know you don't understand that purpose now, but you will. Through your new faith and love in him, his purpose will become clear when the time is right. Remember that when and if you lose your sight, it will be for a very special purpose." He squeezed my hands. "Hold onto that truth and never let go of it. Remember how much he loves you, that in him is all you'll ever need. He has chosen to use you for some very special reason." I so believed and trusted this old man that his words comforted me and brought me peace. I nodded that I understood.

Charlie got up and went inside, saying he'd be back out in a moment. Darkness had set upon us a good while ago. I put more wood on the fire until it burned brightly. Charlie appeared holding two glasses of his special tea and handed me a glass. He truly enjoyed this special drink.

He raised his glass to mine. "To you, Ryan, my dear and trusted friend. May we drink to your safe voyage home. It is time for you to go." Our glasses clinked together as we slowly sipped the heavenly nectar. I stared at Charlie, not sure what to say. This place, his home, had become a special sanctuary to me. It was strange to think of leaving. Finally, I forced out the words, "Are you sure? Am I really ready to go home?"

He smiled, a look of love and kindness in his eyes. "Yes, Ryan, my son. You are ready to go home. You have people who love you waiting for you there. It's time for you to allow them the joy of knowing the new you. Share with them in celebration your rebirth, your new appreciation for the precious gift of life. Welcome them into your arms and they will feel the love and strength of your relationship with God. Oh, the wonderful life that awaits you, son. Hallelujah, thank you God," he shouted into the night air. He was filled with excitement and joy and so was I. He put his arm around my shoulders. "And ask that sweet lady to marry you before she slips away, before she realizes the bum you really are," he said with a wink. We laughed.

We gazed up at the night sky, a night sky unlike any I had seen before. Maybe it was the big sky of Montana, or maybe it was God's gift, allowing me to see beyond my sight.

"Hallelujah, hallelujah," I shouted. "Thank you, Lord, thank you!" Charlie looked at me. "Oh, Charlie, isn't it just beautiful? Isn't it wonderful?" I couldn't hide my excitement. "Never have I seen a star-filled sky like this. Life is truly a miracle and a wonder to behold." I raised my glass. "To my new life in Christ, Charlie."

"To your new life in Christ," he repeated. We spent several hours talking and gazing into the heavens. Several falling stars streaked across the black sky. My thoughts turned to home. Suddenly I was overwhelmed by how much I missed everyone. I couldn't wait to have Sarah in my arms, or to see the smiles and hear the screams of excitement from our children. I truly was a man blessed.

It had been a long day and Charlie had shared so much. I was exhausted. Charlie carried our glasses inside while I put out the fire. I thanked him for a very special day, gave him a hug and bade him good night. I crawled into bed and Red joined me. "Boy, we're going home," I said.

That night I had the most vivid dream. A long straight path stretched before me. In the distance, at what appeared to be the end of the path, shone a brilliant, nearly blinding light. I felt drawn to the light and as I walked toward it, I heard that voice again saying *Stay true to the path I've put you on.* As I drew closer, my eyes adjusted to the brilliance and I could make out two figures. Slowly, one of them stepped forward and the brilliance continued around him, brightly lighting my path. I rubbed my eyes and when I looked again, I saw it was Jesus. He stretched his arms toward me and said, "My precious child, do not fear the path I put you on, for I am always with you, just as I am always with all my precious children who believe in me." Then the other figure stepped forward, beside Jesus, and he put his arm around her. I couldn't believe my eyes. Next to Jesus, wearing that dark flowered dress, was my mother. Joy radiated from her. She smiled and said, "I love you my precious son. Hold close to you the words I shared with you so many years ago. I will always live in your heart. Though my time with you was short, your love filled me with a lifetime of happiness and joy."

In their presence I was filled with a such a deep sense of love and peace. I reached out to touch her but the brilliant light enveloped them and they were gone.

CHAPTER TWENTY-SEVEN

The next day was a mixture of emotions. I was happy at the thought of seeing everyone back home, but sad at leaving this special place and saying farewell to Charlie. The powerful dream I had of seeing Jesus and my mother was still with me and it brought closure to my regrets about losing her. It also strengthened my faith and confidence in continuing my journey.

I savored every precious moment of this day, for I would be heading home tomorrow. On this morning, as we spent time at the altar, we gave prayers of thanks for all of our blessings, and Charlie prayed for my safe passage. We returned to the cabin and did our daily reading. Charlie was even more upbeat than usual.

We drove into town so I could call home with the news. My son screamed with excitement and Sarah burst into tears. I told them I should be home late Friday afternoon and Sarah told me she'd take the day off to prepare for my homecoming. I told her not to plan anything elaborate, that I wanted private time with her and our children. I really was a blessed man. I didn't call work; I figured I would cross that bridge after I returned. At this point, I doubted that a couple days would matter one way or the other.

I purchased some snacks and drinks for my journey and thanked Big Jim for his hospitality and kindness. He gave me a firm handshake and said it had been a pleasure meeting me.

As we drove back to Charlie's place I found myself lost in a sea of thoughts. I had grown to love this place and this dear old man. I knew I would sorely miss him. I wondered how all the changes in me would carry home? Charlie's Woods had been a sacred sanctuary. What would happen with me when I left here I didn't know.

"You're unusually quiet today," Charlie finally said. "Is everything okay?"

"I'm okay. Just a mixed bag of emotions."

"I understand," he replied.

"Charlie, I'm going to miss you."

"And I'll miss you, too. but know that even though we'll be physically apart, spiritually we'll be bound together for the rest of our lives, so you see, we really won't be apart." His words comforted me and I finally smiled back. "That's better," he said. "It is a glorious day."

I laughed. "Yes it is, Charlie." We sang praise songs to the Lord the rest of the way home.

After lunch we walked to the gorge to spend one last afternoon together. We reveled in being alive and just enjoyed the beauty of our surroundings. We watched Red chase birds and butterflies and laughed at his playfulness.

That evening I cooked dinner for a change. Charlie sat back and teased me as I prepared our meal. "Everything is very good," he said, "but I knew it would be."

"I'm glad you enjoyed it," I replied. "How do I ever repay you for all that you've done for me?" He sat there for a moment, rubbing his chin as if deep in thought. He was quiet for the longest time, and when he spoke I was shocked by his words.

"Writing comes pretty natural for you, doesn't it? I mean, it's easy for you to express yourself, your feelings, in words, isn't it?"

"Well, yes," I said. "It was one of my strong points in school and college. Why do you ask?"

"You remember me saying that you were blessed with a gift, and you told me that you had no idea what it was?"

"Yes," I said.

"That's it!" His voice filled with excitement.

"What's it?" I said.

"Write!" His excitement only grew. "Oh, hallelujah, thank you, Lord, and have patience with him, he's just a rookie."

"What in the world are you talking about? Fill me in," I said. His exuberance made me laugh.

"I told you you'd have your answers before you left here," he said. "You are to write for people to read."

"Write what?" I asked. "What could I possibly write that people would want to read?"

"Oh, ye of little faith," he said. "Rookie! Well, first off, you'll have plenty of time since you said you most likely don't have a job."

"Oh, shoot, thanks," I said. "You're really making me feel better." Charlie's sense of humor could come through when you least expected it, but it was always filled with hidden wisdom and truth.

"Faith, Ryan, remember you are on a journey of faith," he said, pointing at me. "Write about your experience here, your thoughts, and your feelings. All of it, Ryan, put it all on paper, put it in a book." He then said something that I wouldn't understand or fully appreciate until later. "This is his purpose for you, the path he wishes you to travel. Remember the voice in your dream: *Trust in me, and stay true to the path I've put you on.* Oh, hallelujah!" he shouted, lifting his eyes to the heavens. "Son, God is guiding your life and your destiny. Now have faith and listen."

He was emphatic. And to my surprise I believed all of it. At this moment I didn't know how, I didn't have a clue, but my dream validated the truth he was telling me. "Son, many, many people will benefit from your experience. Oh, the good that it will do, the seeds of hope it will sow. Glory be to God," he said, closing his eyes. "Glory be to God," he repeated softly. If Charlie believed sharing my experience would truly help people, then I was willing to write about it.

"Son, know that he loves you and watches over you and the Holy Spirit guides you. God doesn't give bad advice," he said with a smile. "Remember, there will be many times along your journey that negative forces will try to distract you from your chosen path and cloud your vision. Do not allow them to throw you off course. Walk steadfastly along your path armed by the power of your faith and the vision of his glory will always be in front of you. If God be for you, then fear nothing that be against you. Remember these words by the apostle Paul to the Romans, for they carry the strength of truth:

For I am persuaded, that neither death, nor life, nor angels, nor principalities, nor powers, nor things present, nor things to come, nor height, nor depth, nor any other creature shall be able to separate us from the love of God, which is in Christ Jesus our Lord.

"Ryan," he said, placing his hands on mine. "Carry these truths forever in your heart. Feel, experience his boundless love for you and all people, strengthen your faith by praying to him every day, take time to be still and listen to his voice. And feed your spirit daily with his word. Do these things and your life will be blessed beyond your wildest dreams."

He paused. "Our work here is finished for now, and you have the answers you sought. Let us pray and give thanks."

As we said *amen*, I felt totally overwhelmed from the evening's events. I sat back in my chair, closed my eyes, taking slow deep breaths, trying to calm myself.

Charlie poured us our last special tea. We spent the rest of the evening reminiscing about our time together. We laughed and we cried.

Finally, he said it was time to retire. He gave me a long hug. "You have a long journey ahead of you, so get a good night's sleep." He said he loved me, then he said good night.

I stared into the fire, still in awe of what had transpired. I was truly heading in a new direction. I could barely believe everything that had occurred over these past two months. I was a lucky man. No, I was *blessed*. And what to make of Charlie? He was unlike anybody I had ever met. I was convinced he had mystical supernatural qualities and yes, as hard as it might be to believe, a direct connection to God. I was tired and pulled the blanket from the rocker. I laid down by the fireplace next to Red, who was already asleep. I pulled the blanket over both of us and we drifted off to sleep.

CHAPTER TWENTY-EIGHT

I didn't awaken until ten the following morning. The fire was a pile of smoldering embers. My aches and pains reminded me that sleeping on the floor had lost the charm it held in my youth. Red greeted me with his usual exuberance, licking my cheek and barking. I opened the door to let him out. There was a strange silence in the cabin. Charlie should have been up hustling about by now. I could smell the aroma of brewing coffee. I washed my face and brushed my teeth, then walked outside to see if I could find Charlie. His truck was gone. *Odd,* I thought. He hadn't told me he was going anywhere.

I let Red back in and walked to the kitchen to pour myself a cup of coffee. There on the counter were some danishes and a note.

Dear Ryan, I apologize for not being able to see you off. Something important came up which needed my attention. It's hard to find the words to express my joy for the time we spent together. I will never forget the special person you are nor the special friendship we share. Please do not be disheartened by my absence. I will cherish forever in my heart the time we spent together. May you share with the world your new life, love, and knowledge of our brotherhood. You will be a ray of light in a dark world. If you stay true to your destiny, have faith, and trust in God your light will be added to millions of others to brighten our world. I will see you again, but not for a while. You are welcome back here any time. Let no obstacle stand in the way of writing your book. Take time every day to be still and visit with God and he will guide you all the way. Please accept the gift I left you in your car as an expression of my love for you. God bless you. Charlie.

I quietly packed my things, struggling to fight back the tears. As I set everything on the porch, Red and I made one last walk to the old man's altar. It wasn't the same without him. I knelt down and gave thanks to God. As we headed back to the cabin, I savored every step, every breath. What a different man I had become. My fears and insecurities had vanished. As I packed the car I knew I would sorely miss the old man and his woods. Though my life had been turned inside out. I now walked with a deep sense of peace and purpose. I yelled thanks and goodbye to Charlie, for part of him was in these woods. I opened the driver's door and Red jumped in. There on my seat was his precious Bible. As I held this special, special book to my chest, I began to cry. "Charlie, why me?" All my emotions and gratitude flowed forth. As I pressed his precious gift to my lips, I felt his presence all around me. I turned, but no one was there. My tears turned to laughter as I thought of the grin that I was sure was on Charlie's face.

I wrapped the Bible in one of my shirts and tucked it carefully in my suitcase. I climbed in, shut the door, and turned the key. As I pulled away, I paused to look back at the cabin that had become my home. "Thank you, Charlie, for showing me a new life." I couldn't help but wonder what the future had in store for me.

ACKNOWLEDGEMENTS

This book would not be complete without expressing my deepest gratitude and appreciation to those special people who helped make it possible.

A special thanks to my dear friend Ken whose faith and belief in me never wavers. He has traveled alongside me in our journey with Christ and his fellowship has been invaluable in helping me keep the faith. His constant support and encouragement keep me writing.

I am grateful to Jim Mitchell who has become a dear, close friend. His faith and belief in me is a constant source of encouragement. A special thanks to his wife, Elaine, who put me in touch with Jason Liller, my editor.

Every good or great book needs a great and talented editor and I found both in Jason. His remarkable talent, commitment, and hard work on this project were invaluable. Jason also knew Charlie Jones in real life which gave him a special insight into my heart as I recreated the essence and powerful dynamic between the character Ryan and the old man Charlie. He is a joy to work with and has helped make me a better writer. I thank God for bringing him into this project. I look forward to doing future projects with him.

To my family and closest friends whose belief in me keeps me writing.

My deepest and most heartfelt gratitude to the love of my life, Veronica, who was the inspiration behind the character of Sarah. She was a wonderful asset as we worked together in editing and making changes to this book. She has been a constant source of encouragement with her endless patience and unfaltering belief in me. She was the rock on this project and also in my life!

ABOUT GEORGE REIKER

George Reiker and his wife Veronica are retired and live in Hanover, Pennsylvania. They have been married twenty-six years and together have four children and four grandchildren. Catch George's *Your Spirit of Power* ministry on Wednesday nights at 8 PM Eastern time on Facebook Live at Facebook.com/george.reiker.5 and on YouTube at bit.ly/georgereiker.

Contact George Reiker at ReikerBooks@Gmail.com.

YOUR SPIRIT OF POWER MINISTRIES

At YOUR SPIRIT OF POWER MINISTRIES our mission is to inspire and empower lives through the love of JESUS CHRIST and the power and guidance of the HOLY SPIRIT, to share the importance of fellowship in love with one another, and to embrace GOD'S divine presence through praise and worship.

Join George Reiker and Your Spirit of Power Ministries on Wednesday nights at 8 PM eastern time on Facebook Live at Facebook.com/george.reiker.5 and on YouTube at bit.ly/georgereiker, or scan the QR code with your smartphone.

WE HOPE TO SEE YOU THERE!

Around the world, many churches have no youth ministry because there is no emphasis on reaching young people for Christ.

GLOBALLEAD IS CHANGING THAT

globalLead has trained youth leaders in 51 countries on 6 continents. Denominations and parachurch ministries utilize globalLead trainers to equip their leaders. globalLead's three tiers of training empower through Jesus-centered principles, Biblical strategies, and goal-setting.

- 90% of churches on most continents have no access to formal theological and ministry training. **globalLead offers ministry-team training to churches.**

- Many pastors and Christian workers are spiritually and relationally drained. **globalLead offers** *Heart of the Leader,* **soul care for the renewal of leaders,** consisting of two one-week seminars, a year apart. Churches have noticed the positive difference in their pastors.

- globalLead impacts an estimated **505,000 people per year,** including indigenous leaders and countries ordinarily closed to the Gospel.

Want to learn more?
Want to invest in empowering believers around the world?
Visit http://globalLead.world and start making a difference today!

Above & Beyond Ministries

leads people into a deeper relationship with the Lord Jesus Christ, accesses uncharted territory, and reaches above and goes beyond human boundaries to fulfill God-given destinies.

Pastor Garry Shaeffer has been ministering to us for twenty-five years. To hear him preach, or to be ministered to personally, is to feel the powerful presence of the Holy Spirit!
—George Reiker

Pastor Garry and Wanda Shaeffer, fifty-year ministry veterans, bring excitement and an expectancy for the Body of Christ to experience the fullness of the Holy Spirit to small and large groups, church services, events, and conferences. You can expect...

- preaching the Word
- teaching the Word
- healing
- people set free from bondages and strongholds
- encouragement and uplifting of local pastors and leaders
- edification and encouragement of the Body of Christ
- support of leaders and their authority in challenging situations and transitions

Above & Beyond Ministries commits to tapping into the awesome power of God, enabling the Bride of Christ to experience and operate in His supernatural power by preaching the Word of God, creating an atmosphere for the releasing of the fullness of the Holy Spirit, and seeing Scripture fulfilled through signs, wonders, and miracles, resulting from a deeper intimate relationship with Him.

Contact Paster Garry Shaeffer today to learn how Above & Beyond Ministries can help you and your group.

Phone: 717-334-2647 or 717-465-5130

315 Crooked Creek Rd. Gettysburg, PA 17325

Made in the USA
Middletown, DE
07 June 2021